ICON

a novel

by Georgia Briggs

Chesterton, Indiana

Pen-and-ink drawings by Georgia Briggs

Published by:
Ancient Faith Publishing
A Division of Ancient Faith Ministries
P.O. Box 748
Chesterton, IN 46304

ISBN: 978-1-944967-19-2

Author photo courtesy of Kara Grace Photography

30 29 28 27 26 25 24 23 22 21   14 13 12 11 10 9 8 7 6 5 4 3

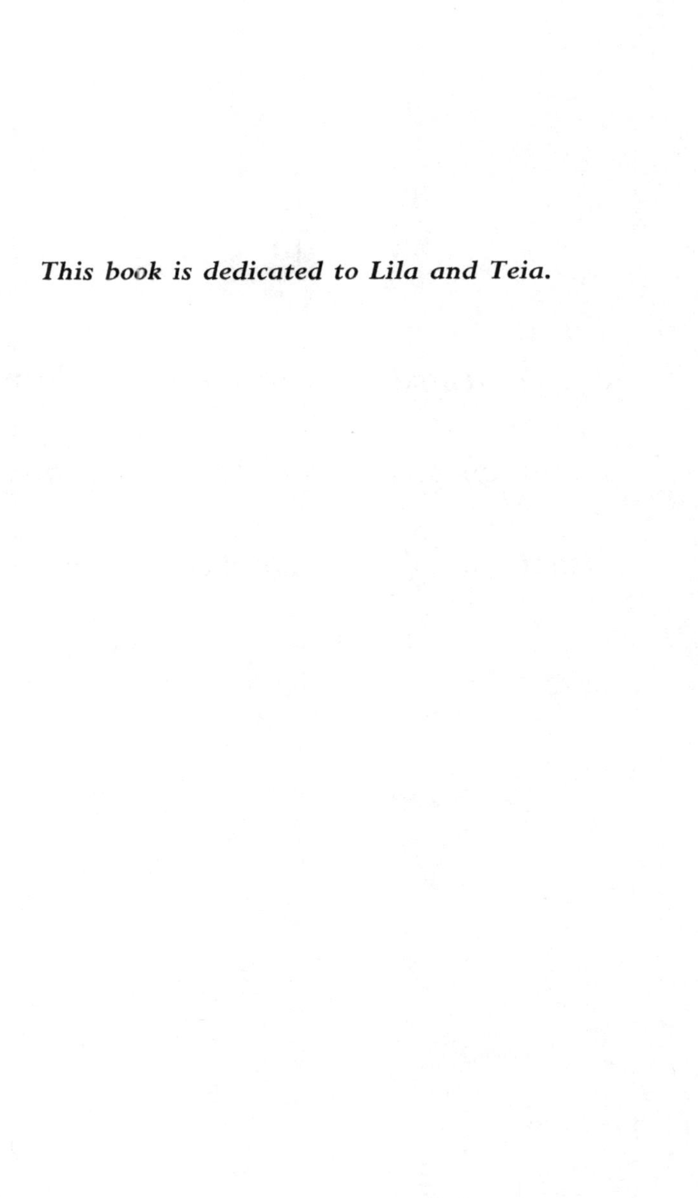

This book is dedicated to Lila and Teia.

ΙϹ | ΟΝ

So God created Man in His own eikona;

in the eikona of God He created him;

male and female He created them.

GENESIS 1:27

ONE

December 3, 0000 Era of Tolerance

"Hillary Matthews, can you stay after class for a moment?"

I freeze in the middle of putting my binder away. Around me everyone else is loud, distracted, ready to go to lunch.

"Hillary?" Miss Linda says again.

I nod to her and zip up my backpack.

The other kids jostle and push their way out the door, hurrying to their lockers or the bathrooms. I lag behind. Miss Linda seems friendly, but she scares me. She looks at me too much. I think she might know.

When I come up to her desk, she's got a piece of paper in her hand. My stomach relaxes. It's just my quiz on Spanish verbs from yesterday. Did I get a bad grade? That's weird. I'm usually pretty good at Spanish.

"Hillary," she says gently in that soft, creepy voice grownups use. "You did so well on your quiz. The best grade in the class."

Something's wrong with her voice. It's not a "congratulations" voice. I scan the quiz she hands me—no words wrong, a perfect score—then my eyes stop on my name at the top of the page.

"Hillary, can you tell me why you signed it like this?" Miss Linda whispers.

In my own neat cursive at the top are the words "Euphrosyne Matthews." I swallow hard. I must not have been thinking. I definitely wrote it myself; there's the little extra loop I always add at the bottom of the *y*.

I feel my stomach tighten again and my heart begin to pound. "I'm sorry," is all I can whisper back.

"Don't worry about it, just don't let it happen again." She takes the quiz out of my shaking hands and shuffles it into her stack of papers, knocking them against the desk so the edges are all lined up neatly.

"I won't," I say. I back away from the desk, edging towards the door. Maybe that's all. Maybe she'll let it go . . .

"Hillary?" she says before I can turn the doorknob. "You live with your grandparents, right?"

She knows.

"Yes, ma'am."

"Richard and Gladys?"

"Yes, ma'am." She even knows their names? Do all the teachers? Do they know where I live? I feel my breath coming faster and try not to panic.

Miss Linda makes a note to herself on a Post-it. "And they . . . they call you Hillary?"

"Yes, ma'am."

"Always?"

"Yes, ma'am." I keep repeating myself. I can hear how scared I sound.

"Good. Good." Miss Linda puts the Post-it on her box of paperclips and gives me a wave. "Well, go on and enjoy your lunch! We'll see you tomorrow."

I open the door and slip out quickly. *We'll see you*, she said. They're all watching me. They all know.

Holy Saturday

It is 6:54 pm, and we are all asleep in our beds. Katerina and my cousin Olivia and I have our white dresses on already so we can roll out of bed and get in the car when it's time to leave. All the fans are on, whirring, blocking out the noise of cars pulling up in the driveway.

I wake up to Hershey whining at the bedroom door. His hearing is better than mine—I still don't know that anything's wrong. I think he has to go potty or something.

Katerina and Olivia are still asleep, Olivia hogging all the blankets next to me. Sighing, I get up, shuffle to the door, and follow the clicking of Hershey's nails into the living room. He runs to the front door, panting expectantly.

There are dark silhouettes against the white curtains. The doorknob rattles.

I stop.

I hear the whine and splinter of wood from outside.

Mom and Dad's room is at the other end of the house. I run down the hall and past my room, tripping over the two stairs in the dark. I scramble up again, ignoring the pain in my shin.

"Dad! Someone's breaking in, I'm scared—"

Mom rubbing her eyes, Dad lurching out of bed, stumbling, grabbing the baseball bat from behind his dresser.

Yelling.

Boots.

Smashing glass.

"Get under the bed!"

"Kat and Olivia—"

"Get under the bed! Hold this."

A small, hard square is pushed into my hands. Dust from the carpet. Family photo albums. A forgotten sock.

"Alex—"

Gunshots.

More glass.

"Please, no—have mercy, Lord have mercy, Theotokos—"

"Not them, please, don't—"

Gunshots.

A dog whimpering.

Boots.

Silence.

December 4, 0000 ET

My room in Grandma and Grandpa's house is clean. And white. There aren't many toys. I used to have a lot of toys, but I got most of them when I was little. I missed them after I came here but didn't feel like buying new ones. What would I do with toys? Sit on the floor and stare at them by myself?

Most of the time I'm okay. It's kind of sad at night when I want to hold onto my old stuffed monkey while I fall asleep. I used to always lie on my stomach with my face turned toward him and my arm wrapped around him. I tried lying on my stomach when I first came here, but without Monkey to prop my arm up, I couldn't get comfortable. So I sleep on my side now. Curled in a little ball, like a roly-poly.

There is a bed with a light blue blanket and a desk made of dark wood. Blinds, which I like to close and open when I'm bored. And a clock on the wall.

The clock is the only thing I've added. I asked Grandma if we could get one the week after I moved in, and she took me to Walmart to pick one out.

I chose a plain one, black-rimmed with a white face and a red second hand.

"Don't you want a digital one?" Grandma was surprised.

"No, I like this one," I said, grabbing the box from the shelf and looking at the price. It wasn't expensive.

"Are you sure? This one doesn't even have an alarm."

"I like this one," I repeated.

Grandpa put a nail in the wall above my bed and hung it up for me. At night I lie here curled on my side and listen to the loud ticking. I don't think as much about the silence. Kat used to snore.

Pascha

I stay under the bed. So long that I pee myself, ruining my white dress. And I still don't come out. I clutch the little wooden square Mom shoved into my hands. I don't even know what it is, but I squeeze it so hard my fingers hurt.

Dad's cell phone starts to buzz. It must have fallen off his bedside table, because I can see it light up on the floor a few feet away. The letters on the screen say "Mark."

Mr. Liakos. Dad's best friend and a reader at church.

I uncurl my fingers from the wooden square and pull the phone under the bed beside me. It's still ringing. I swipe my thumb across the touch-screen to answer it.

"Hello?" I whisper.

"Alex?" comes Mr. Liakos's voice, all muffled and small.

I feel tears well up in my eyes.

"Alex? Are you there?"

I make myself say something. "This is Euphrosyne."

"Sweetie! Can I talk to your dad?"

The tears start to flow. I am sobbing into the phone.

"Euphrosyne. Sweetie. Is your dad there? Are you guys okay?"

"I'm scared to come out," I cry, "I'm scared! I don't want to come out. I think I'm the only one—"

"Did they come? Sweetie, tell me what happened."

"There were men with guns," I sob, "and Mom told me to get under the bed, and Dad went, and I heard shots, and I think I'm the only one . . ."

"Stay where you are. I'm on my way."

"Okay," I whimper.

The screen lights up for a moment to show that the call is disconnected. And then I'm in the dark again. I lie still and try not to think about anything.

Sometime later, I don't know how long, I hear movement. Someone walks down the hallway toward the bedroom. A blue light runs across the floor, tumbling over the folds in a twisted blanket and one of Hershey's toys.

"Euphrosyne?" comes Mr. Liakos's voice. There is the flick of a switch, and the bedroom light comes on. The yellow fluorescence seems sickly. It's still dark outside.

Mr. Liakos's shiny black shoes appear. Church shoes. Then he is on his hands and knees to search under the bed. I still haven't moved.

"There you are, sweetie," he says. "Are you okay?"

I nod.

"Can you come out? It's not safe here. We've got to move."

I start to wiggle my way out from under the bed. I'm all dusty, and my dress is wet and cold with pee.

Mr. Liakos offers me his hand and helps me up. He looks at the square in my hand. "You'll want to hang onto that," he says. He grabs the green blanket off Mom and Dad's bed and wraps it around me. Then he bends down to look me in the eyes.

"It's pretty bad," he says quietly. "If you want, I can carry you, and you can close your eyes till we're outside."

I shake my head. I have pee all over me. And I don't like being hugged or touched by anybody but Mom and Dad.

"Okay," he says. "You just keep your eyes on my back."

The rest of the house is dark, so I only see the dim outlines of things in the blue light cast by Mr. Liakos's phone. I should obey him and keep my eyes forward. But I don't. And some of it I would have seen anyway.

Mom crumpled by the bedroom door.

Two little girls, one in each bed, silent and still.

A broken shadowbox on the floor, two wedding crowns ripped out and trampled.

Splintered icons.

Dad and Hershey are in the living room, Dad face down with Hershey curled up next to him, blood on his nose.

I follow Mr. Liakos out into the night just as a faint, pink glow appears on the eastern horizon. It is Pascha morning. *Christ is Risen.*

December 5, 0000 ET

Afternoons at the library are one of my favorite parts of the day. Grandma picks me up after school and we go to the Nolan C. Mayhew library downtown. She reads another chapter in *Prairie Passion: A Love Story*, and I wander around and look at books. I like the librarians here. They'll help you if you ask for it, but they don't mind you wandering around on your own, as long as you don't take the little kids' bean bag chairs and drag them to the young adult section.

One of the librarians is especially nice. Her name is Mimi. I knew her from before. Her nametag used to say "Mary," which was a pretty common name but one of the first ones to go. I don't know if they assigned her "Mimi," or if she chose it because it sounded close to her old name.

The name changes ended up being more trouble than anybody expected, I think. When they started sorting through them, there were way more that came from saints or people in the Bible than they had realized. And not as many options for new ones as they had hoped. In the end people started using last names, or naming their kids after plants or famous people or places. There's another Hillary in my class, a Boston, a Poppy, three Carters, and one kid named Sheeran.

But anyway, Mimi is nice to me. She helps me find good stuff to read, even though I've already gone through most of the books in the children's section with interesting covers.

Mimi was the one who introduced me to the nonfiction aisles. I had never been interested in those books before, since they didn't have stories. But now I need to know things that I can't ask grownups, or look up on the Internet, since my computer time at school is monitored. Finding stuff in books is a lot slower, but I can do it in private. I've gotten really good at using indexes.

Sometimes I wonder about Mimi. Mary was a common name, so that doesn't really mean anything. Neither does not having any tattoos.

I watch her put books back on the shelves from behind my copy of *The Giver*. She is humming, swaying back and forth so her flowy red skirt swings gently from side to side. She raises her right hand to push back her bangs, and I catch a glint of gold on her ring finger.

I turn the next page of my book and settle a little deeper into the beanbag I'm sitting on. I'll have to keep an eye on Mimi.

Pascha

Mr. Liakos and I drive for a long time in his green truck. I huddle in the blanket. It's not cold, but the feeling of the thick, knitted material wrapped tightly around me is comforting. For the first time I feel safe enough to cry. So I do. I curl up in a tiny ball and lean against the door. On the dashboard, a mounted icon of the Theotokos shakes as we bounce over railroad crossings. The neon letters of the clock say 4:55.

Mr. Liakos is nice enough to just let me cry and not tell me it will be okay. All he does is take one hand off of the steering wheel and give my shoulder a squeeze.

We're taking country roads, weaving between fields of uncut grass and scraggly pine trees. After a little while, Mr. Liakos says, "I'm not really sure where I'm going."

"Shouldn't we go to the police station?" I say through my tears. My voice comes out high and babyish.

Mr. Liakos shakes his head. "It's not safe."

Not safe to go to the police? What's happening? I feel even more terrified than before. I grasp the wooden square harder.

"Euphrosyne," says Mr. Liakos, "Did you see the people who broke into your house?"

I shake my head. "I only heard them."

"Almost all of the families at St. John's have been attacked tonight. That's why I called your dad, to see if you all were okay. You live farther from the city than most people, so I thought I might reach you in time for you to get out."

"But why can't we go to the police?" I ask him. I'm not even getting what he's saying. That most of the people I know are dead.

"The police set the church on fire."

"What?"

I can't even imagine someone setting St. John's on fire. It's so silent and beautiful when you walk in, with its white walls and domed ceiling and the thick, holy smell of incense. And the saints staring at you from the icons on the walls. All those icons. Are they burning? I feel lost. The two places in the world that I thought would never change—home and St. John's—are gone.

Mr. Liakos sniffs, and I see that his eyes are shiny too. The church is his world. He and his family are there for every service.

"Is your family okay?" I ask him.

He just shakes his head. He's staring hard at the road,

and I wonder if he even believes what's happened yet.

"Daniel's in Austria on a college trip," he says after a moment. His voice sounds strained. "He might be all right. I haven't been able to get in touch with him yet. And I don't know what I'll say to him when I do."

I imagine Daniel, far away in another country, finding out that his mother is gone, that he's an only child.

I'm an only child. I'm an orphan. I feel my throat tighten and my eyes start to water again. What were the last things I said to Kat and Olivia? I can't even remember. Was it telling them to stop hogging the sink so I could brush my teeth? I'm a terrible person. I bury my face in my hands.

We drive and drive, and I fall asleep crying. When I wake up, I have a bad taste in my mouth, and my neck hurts from leaning against the truck's fake wood paneling. It's light out, 7:22 am, and the truck is stopping. That's what wakes me up. I raise my head and look around groggily. We're in a McDonald's parking lot.

"I need to eat something and go to the bathroom," says Mr. Liakos. "Are you hungry?"

"Yeah," I say. And I really have to pee. I unwrap my blanket to unbuckle my seatbelt. I look pretty gross. My white dress is stained and smelly, and my hair is all over the place. I don't have shoes.

For the first time I notice that Mr. Liakos looks bad too. He has his reader's cassock on over his church clothes, but the black cloth has a rip at the neck and some dark stains on the side. His eyes are kind of red and have grey circles underneath them. He smells like incense and smoke.

We look at each other a minute, and Mr. Liakos says, "I think they'll call the cops if we go in there like this."

"Probably," I agree.

"There's a brush under your seat somewhere," Mr. Liakos says. "And I can take off this cassock." He pulls it off, struggling in the cramped space, folds it carefully, and stows it in the glove compartment. Underneath it he has on a white polo shirt and a pair of khaki pants. Normal enough, except that there's some red on the side of his shirt. I guess the dark stuff on the cassock was blood.

I find the brush and get my hair under control. I still feel gross.

"Keep the blanket wrapped around you like you're sleepy, and maybe no one will notice," says Mr. Liakos.

"Okay. You've got some blood on your shirt," I say.

"I'll try and keep it covered up with my arm."

We get out of the truck. My legs are wobbly from being bent for so long. It's exactly like early morning road trips— stopping at McDonald's, the pink sunlight filtering through the clouds, hungry and sleepy—except that I'm with Mr. Liakos instead of Mom, Dad, and Kat. Except that everything is wrong.

The McDonald's is almost empty inside. The only other customers are a man in paint-stained overalls and an elderly couple having a pancake breakfast at one of the corner booths. The lady behind the counter doesn't even look up as we come in. She's got triple ear piercings and is sneakily texting behind the register.

"Let's go to the bathroom first," Mr. Liakos whispers to me. "I need to wash my face and hands."

I nod, wishing I had a toothbrush so I could get this taste out of my mouth.

The girls' bathroom is dirty and smells like hand soap. I use the toilet quickly, hanging up my blanket on the door so it doesn't drag in the patches of hopefully-water on the brown tiled floor. I try to avoid stepping in those with my bare feet. When I'm done, I dab my damp pair of underwear with toilet paper. It doesn't do much good. I wince as I pull them up and they stick to my legs.

My reflection in the bathroom mirror makes me pause as I'm washing my hands. Maybe it's the weird yellow-green light overhead, but my skin looks the wrong color. Too grey. My eyes are puffy and sad. I splash some warm water on my face and look around for a paper towel. There's only one of those useless air-dryer things.

Mr. Liakos's face is also dripping a little when he comes out of the men's room. He looks more awake, though. "Come on, let's get something to eat," he says.

We walk up to the counter and look at the menu.

"How can I help you?" the girl behind the counter says, still eyeing her phone.

"Just give us one minute, please," says Mr. Liakos.

I'm debating between oatmeal and hash browns when I remember that I can get whatever I want. Lent is over.

"Remember, we can have meat now," Mr. Liakos says to me quietly, evidently thinking the same thing. "But it needs to be something you can eat in the car."

Mom and Dad were planning on taking us to Cracker Barrel to break the fast. I was going to get eggs and sausage and waffles. I want to start crying again, even though it's stupid to cry over waffles when almost everybody you know is dead. But the McDonald's lady is looking suspiciously at our dirty clothes and tired faces, so I clench my hands until my nails dig into my palms, and then I focus on the menu and forget about crying.

"Do you know what you want?" Mr. Liakos asks me. He's noticed the lady's stare and now he's started shifting uncomfortably from one foot to the other.

"An Egg McMuffin and an orange juice," I say.

"We'll have that and two sausage biscuits and a large diet Coke to go."

She punches it into the register. "Just swipe right there," she says, tapping the credit card machine with a long, gold fingernail.

Mr. Liakos swipes his card and goes to fill up his drink. I stand by the corner, sipping at the orange juice that the lady hands me. It's not doing much for the taste in my mouth.

The food doesn't take very long, but waiting around with the lady staring at us makes me nervous. I'm relieved when Mr. Liakos hands me the warm paper sack and we can get back to the truck.

Mr. Liakos eats his sausage biscuits one at a time and drives with his knees. I hold my sandwich for a few minutes before I bite into it, just feeling its warmth. The meat tastes so good. When I'm done, my fingers are all greasy. I wipe them off on a napkin and then pull the wooden square out from under my seat. "Do you know where we're going yet?" I ask Mr. Liakos.

"I have an idea," he says. "I want to check on Father Innocent. He's had some health problems, so he hasn't been able to make it to church lately. If he's okay, he might know what's going on and where we can go."

"Okay," I say, trying to remember what Father Innocent looks like. I've heard Mom and Dad talk about him before, but I can't picture his face.

"We're about an hour away," Mr. Liakos says. "He has a trailer out in the country. Might've been overlooked."

That's what you thought about us, I think. I hope Mr. Liakos is right this time.

The meat makes my stomach feel full, and I'm starting to get sleepy again. I wrap the blanket back around me, fold my arms over the wooden square, and close my eyes.

I don't sleep very well because of the bumpy road. But I must have dozed off at least a little, because when the truck stops suddenly, the clock on the dashboard says 8:41. Mr. Liakos is talking fast—what is he saying? I feel so disoriented, and my stomach is not happy about the Egg McMuffin.

"Euphrosyne. Euphrosyne, I need you to stay curled up like that, okay? I'm going to ask what's going on, but don't get out unless it's safe. Okay? Hold onto that icon. Say, 'Lord Jesus Christ, have mercy on me.' Just keep saying it."

"What? What's going on?"

"Just keep saying it," he says, opening the truck door. He unbuckles his seatbelt and steps out, grinning confidently, just like he does when he's meeting new people at church. "Well, hello there!" I hear his muffled voice from outside. "Is the road blocked?"

"Driver's license, please," I hear another man say.

"Sure, just give me a second to find it . . ."

"Is that blood on your shirt?"

"Ha, no, ketchup. Had to make a breakfast run to McDonald's and that packet practically exploded on me—"

A lower voice speaks up, sounding suspicious. "What is that around his neck?"

"Show us the necklace," says the first voice.

There's a moment of silence. I sit perfectly still, my heart beating, my fingers wrapped around the three-bar cross hanging from my own neck.

"He's one of them," the low voice says. "Shoot him."

Before I have time to even realize what's happening, there's a crack of sound that makes me jump.

"Check his pockets and his phone," says the first voice. "Then go through the vehicle. He might have names, contacts."

I slowly raise my head over the dashboard. A Jeep is pulled across the road ahead, blocking both lanes. Two men are bending over a body on the ground.

I pull the handle of the door gently. It clicks open. Neither man turns around. They've found his wallet and are looking through it, tossing cards and receipts on the ground.

I slither out of the truck and press the door almost shut. I run for the woods, clutching the icon.

December 6, 0000 ET

"Hillary, what are you doing still sleeping?"

I lie facing the wall with my knees pulled up against my chest. It's 7:15. I have to be at school by 7:55.

"I told you we should have gotten that digital clock with the alarm. Hurry up, you're going to be late!" Grandma says.

"I'm not feeling good," I say. "I can't go to school today."

"Hmm." She comes over and feels my forehead. Her hands are soft and smell like the dryer sheets she always uses. She's not a bad person. She's just not my parents.

"You don't have a fever," she says. "What's wrong? Stomachache?"

"I just don't feel good," I say again.

"Well, unless something's wrong, you have to go to school. I think you'll be okay." She gives me two little comforting pats. "You get dressed quickly, and I'll heat you up one of those sausage biscuits your Grandpa got."

I don't want to eat sausage. It's December, I think. But I nod so that I won't hurt her feelings.

And I get out of bed so that I don't hurt her feelings. And put on my jeans and a sweater. She really tries. How could she know? I pull on my fluffy socks, the ones I wear when I'm sad.

"Hillary?" Grandma calls from the other room.

"Ma'am?"

"Why are your shoes by the front door? You know the rule about putting things away."

"Sorry. I forgot," I lie. My sneakers are where I left them the night before, looking very lonely and sorry for themselves.

I shake them upside down before I put them on, just in case. St. Nicholas has not left me anything. And then I'm upset and mad at myself. Stupid. Of course they're empty. I eat my stupid sausage biscuit and tell my stupid self to enjoy it.

December 7, 0000 ET

On Thursdays I go to see Dr. Snead. Grandma drives me over after school, and we sit in the waiting room until he comes and takes me back to his office. I don't like the waiting room. It's always way too warm, and the dark brown walls make me feel claustrophobic. The plants on the walnut end tables are fake, probably because there are no windows and they'd shrivel up and die if they were real. The chairs look nice, but they make you sit up too straight, and the arm rails are too high. It's the kind of waiting room that's supposed to be all comfortable and homey-looking but makes you feel like you're suffocating.

"Hillary?"

I look up from *The Giver.* Dr. Snead is standing in front of me, carrying my file under one arm.

"I'll see you in a little bit, sweetie," says Grandma.

I follow Dr. Snead into the back. There are lots of offices, some of them with the doors closed and little white-noise—

makers running outside them. Dr. Snead's office is second to last.

"Have a seat," he says, switching his noise-maker on and shutting the door behind us.

I sit on the leather couch, gripping my book. I like carrying a book around with me so that I have something to do with my hands.

Dr. Snead sits in his swivel chair, crosses his legs, and opens my file. "So how are you today?" he asks.

"Good," I say, just like I always do.

He nods, flipping through pages. "I see you had a pretty good week at school."

"Yeah."

I wonder how long it has been since Dr. Snead was in seventh grade. I can't imagine him wearing anything but pinstripe pants and vest and his running shoes, which is what he wears every week. He'd get made fun of for that in my school.

He stops flipping through the pages and lifts a piece of paper, dropping his chin to peer at it over his bifocals.

I clutch my book tighter.

"I see Miss Linda made a note on your Spanish quiz," he says. He puts the paper on his desk and keeps shuffling the others. "Do you often write the wrong name down when you're not thinking?"

"No," I say.

Dr. Snead *hmms*. He takes a few other papers out of my file and lays them beside the Spanish quiz.

"Come have a look at these for me," he says.

I get up from the couch and stand by the desk to see. The other papers are random—a math worksheet, a vocab quiz, and the first page of my reading test. They're all signed *Hillary*. I don't know how I could get in trouble for these.

"I'd like you to take a look at your handwriting here," Dr. Snead says, pushing his glasses back up on his nose. "We can tell a lot about people through handwriting, you know."

I don't say anything, just scan the papers. They aren't messy or anything.

"Compare the writing on the mistake on your Spanish quiz to your signatures on the other papers," he says. He points a thick finger to the cursive *Euphrosyne*, with its fancy looped *y*, then points to the square, all-capital letters of *Hillary*. "See the difference?"

I nod, afraid of where he's going with this.

"I'm concerned, Hillary," he says, scooping the papers up again and tucking them away in my file. He stares at me without blinking. "I'm concerned that you still aren't comfortable with who Hillary is. You haven't taken ownership of Hillary yet."

I look down at my book. "I'm fine," I say.

"I think it would benefit you to practice writing your name, develop a signature that's your own. Get comfortable with yourself. I'm going to give you some homework this week to work on your autograph."

"Okay," I say. I sit back down on the couch.

He sighs deeply and sets the file on his desk. "It's often very hard for people who have come out of cults or oppressive communities to find their own voice and their own personalities right away. But you're a strong girl. I think if you give it time, you can move beyond what you've been through and build a new life.

"Does that make you upset?" he goes on. "I noticed that you pull on your fingers like that when you're anxious."

"I'm fine," I say again.

"Hillary, it's normal to have a hard time with all this, especially at your age. I'm sure you loved your family very much."

I nod.

"And what happened to them was a tragedy. But what we can learn from this is that closed-mindedness and judging others leads to violence. We have to move beyond black-and-white thinking and learn to accept everyone."

I look at the old man on the cover of my book. Those people lived in a black-and-white world. But wasn't that because they got rid of stuff like love and anger that lead to violence? It seems like the opposite of what Dr. Snead is saying.

"It's so hard to understand at your age, I know," he goes on. "But try and think of how far you've come. When you first started seeing me, you were refusing to eat meat on Wednesdays and Fridays! Isn't it more freeing to have all types of food open to you? Life is like that. If you let yourself get tied down by other people's restrictions, you end up missing a lot of the best things. The really important thing is to accept others and yourself for whatever brings you happiness."

But I'm not happy, I think.

"Just think about it," says Dr. Snead. "Accepting yourself

as Hillary doesn't mean betraying your family's memory. You can love them and miss them and still form your own views about what it means to be a good person."

We sit silently for a minute. I don't want to talk to him. I never want to be here.

"Will you think about it for me?" he asks.

"I don't know," I say.

"Well, it's up to you. I think it could help a lot."

Pascha

The trees are scraggly, and I'm afraid the men will see me before I can get far enough away. The ground hurts my bare feet. I'm too scared to look back. When they search the truck, they'll see two McDonald's cups. A blanket in the passenger seat. They'll know. Any minute they'll run after me and shoot me.

Mr. Liakos is dead.

Mr. Liakos is dead.

I scramble up a hill, half-slipping on the leaves, and run down the other side. I need to find a place to hide. I can't outrun a grownup. My heart pounds, and I'm afraid I'm going to pee myself again.

I hear shouts behind me. I pause and look around for something—anything—that can hide me. Nothing. Only trees. Not even thick ones I can hide behind. I can hear someone crashing through the brush, coming in my direction.

I'm so scared. I just want it to be over. Please don't let it hurt. Please don't let it hurt. Lord Jesus Christ have mercy on me. Lord Jesus Christ have mercy on me. Please let me wake up, please let it be a nightmare, make it stop, please make it stop . . .

"Got her!"

I wheel around, holding up the icon instinctively in front of me.

There's another *crack* of sound, this time so loud my ears feel like they've split. Something slams into my chest, knocking me backwards and onto the ground. The whole world is silent except for a high-pitched hum. I lie still in the dirt and leaves, not moving. Maybe I'm dead.

It's a long time before I move again. The humming slowly fades, and I can hear the wind rustling the leaves, an occasional bird chirping. My chest hurts like someone punched me. I keep my eyes shut and hope I'll hear Mom's voice. Maybe she's here.

But no voice comes. An ant or mosquito or something bites me on the ankle. Finally I open my eyes.

I'm still in the woods. Late morning sun streams through the leaves overhead. What happened to the man chasing me? I sit up, feeling dizzy, and look around.

The wood is empty. He's gone. What happened? Was I shot? I touch my chest. It hurts pretty bad, but there's no blood or anything. Not anywhere on me. Only my hands are scraped up for some reason, almost like the time we did tug-of-war on field day at school and I got that rope burn.

My ankle itches. I scratch it hard. I can't figure out what happened.

I was running, and then I stopped. I heard someone coming, but there was nowhere to hide. He yelled something, and I turned around and held up the icon . . . wait, where's the icon?

I stand up and scan the ground. There it is—a few feet away, lying face up by a fallen pine tree. I go to get it, and then I stop.

It's an icon of St. Nicholas, my mother's patron saint, the icon she always kept on her bedside table. He stands calmly in front of his gold background, one hand wrapped around a Bible, the other making the sign of blessing. His face is unchanged, serious and quiet, but lodged in his painted chest, right between the two blue crosses on his stole, is a bullet.

My hands shake as I reach to pick the icon up. It's small and light in my hands. I turn it sideways. It's only about a quarter of an inch thick, but the bullet hasn't gone all the way through. From the back it looks fine, *Nicole Matthews* written in black marker on the left-hand corner. I turn it around again.

I was holding it in front of me when he fired the gun. Right in front of my chest. It must have stopped the bullet, and the force blew it through my hands and knocked me over. Did the man think I was dead?

I sit back down on the ground and gaze at the icon. St. Nicholas looks so calm. The bullet in his chest bothers me. I start to pick at it with my fingernails, trying to pry it loose. A rock I find by a tree root gives me better leverage.

It's wedged in tightly, but after a few minutes I manage to work it out.

A thin trickle of blood runs from the hole in the saint's chest.

"How did you like it?" Mimi says with a smile.

"It was really good, but also kind of sad," I say, handing her *The Giver*.

She holds the book up and runs a finger across the old man's face. That's part of why I read the books she gives me. I know she loves each one.

"Yeah, it is kind of sad," she says as she scans the book in and puts it on the cart behind her desk. "I wish she had written more at the end, so we could tell if things turned out okay for Jonas and Gabe."

"I know," I say. "I couldn't tell if he was dreaming or if he really made it somewhere safe. Why didn't the writer just make it obvious?"

"Maybe she thought it was more realistic this way," says Mimi. "Life is full of cliff-hangers. Things don't always wrap up neatly."

"That's why books should end well," I say. "There's too much sadness in real life already."

Mimi laughs. "The older you get, the more that's true."

How reassuring.

Mimi leans her elbows on the desk and rests her chin in her palms. The ring on her right hand glitters. "I have another book for you to read, if you like. It's kind of sad at the beginning, but it has a happy ending. It's one of my favorites."

I grin. She always says every book that she recommends is her favorite. "Yeah! What's it about?"

"It's about a girl who's depressed because of something bad that happened to her. She's in ninth grade, and she's lonely, so she's got to figure out how to get past what happened. It sounds sad, but parts of it are actually really funny. It describes high school perfectly." Mimi gets up and leads me back to the young adult section.

I think of school, where Miss Linda watches me and the other kids don't talk to me, and it sounds all too familiar.

"Anderson . . . Anderson . . ." Mimi mutters to herself. She scans the book spines, looking for the right name.

"I think I might be depressed sometimes," I say. I don't know why I say it. I don't know the librarian that well.

For a minute Mimi doesn't answer. Then she says, "Me too." She pulls a book from the shelf and hands it to me. The cover has a girl's face partially covered by the branches of a silver tree. "Here. It's called *Speak*. You'll have to let me know what you think. Especially about Melinda's trees."

"Her what?"

"You'll see."

I look at the cover, and Mimi looks around, as though she doesn't want to go back and sit behind her desk. She fingers her ring absentmindedly.

"Hey, Mimi?"

"Yeah?"

"Why do you wear your wedding ring on your right hand?"

She stops playing with it and gives me a considering look. I know that look—grownups make it when they're trying to decide whether to tell you something.

"That's the hand I use to make promises with," she says. She watches me carefully.

"I used to know . . . some people . . . who did that," I whisper.

Mimi nods. She glances around, but no one is near us. "I'll tell you what," she says. "You read *Speak*. And when you come back we'll talk about trees."

December 10, 0000 ET

It's Sunday morning, which means the TV is on. New episodes of every TV show air on Sundays now. Grandma and Grandpa are watching the latest episode of *Saved by Santa*, which is basically about Santa Claus going to different parents that are all judgmental and strict and teaching them to accept their kids no matter what.

Mom and Dad probably wouldn't have let me watch this show. The teenage kids do a lot of stuff that's embarrassing to see with your grandparents, and Santa Claus is actually an old lady, which would have made them mad. But I'm tired of sitting in my bedroom and it's raining outside, so I sit in Grandpa's leather recliner and write *Hillary* over and over on a notepad. Maybe if I do this Dr. Snead will stop asking me questions.

I try writing it lots of different ways, sometimes in cursive, sometimes in the big bubbly letters that the popular girls write with, even with little hearts for the dot in the 'i.' In the end I get frustrated and go back to writing it in blocky capital letters.

It's not my name. I've written it so many times that the letters don't even make sense anymore. I tear out the sheets of paper I've wasted and crumple them up.

The noise makes Grandpa look over. "You okay there, Hillie-billie?" he asks in his gruff voice. "Having trouble with that math again?"

"I don't know," I mutter. *I'm not Hillie-billie.* "I'm gonna go upstairs and read for a little bit."

"That's a good idea, give yourself a break," says Grandpa, turning his attention back to the TV.

I crawl out of the recliner and head upstairs as Santa Claus pulls off her fake beard and starts to put on lipstick.

TWO

Antipascha

"Mr. and Mrs. Matthews?"

"Yes, ma'am, that's us," my Grandpa says.

"You've filled out all the forms?"

"Yes, ma'am, except we weren't sure what to put here under 'name' . . ."

"Let me look that up for you. What's her social? Oh yes. Um . . . I have it here as 'Hillary Jane.' Just make sure to print so we can read it."

Grandpa writes it in with the fountain pen that he always carries around with him and then hands the stack of papers back to the woman at the desk.

"Thank you. She's right in there, but don't leave yet. I think Dr. Snead wants to see you before you go. He'll be her regular therapist."

"Is she okay?" I hear Grandma whisper.

"I'm sure she'll be fine," the lady says. "Dr. Snead will fill you in."

I'm sitting in the next room on a blue vinyl couch, wrapped up in a blanket and staring at my feet. They're still bare and dirty. I have on different clothes—an extra-large T-shirt and boys' basketball shorts—but they couldn't find any shoes for me. My brain feels kind of numb, and I keep thinking about how I wish I could have shoes. And a shower.

Grandma and Grandpa come in. Grandma gives me a big hug. "Are you okay, honey?" she asks.

I nod. I don't even know them that well. They never talked to Mom and Dad. Why are they being all nice to me now?

"Lady at the desk says your name's gonna be Hillary," Grandpa says, sitting down beside me. "Must be nice to have a name people will be able to spell, huh?" He winks at me.

"Richard," Grandma murmurs.

"What?" he says. "I'm just saying."

Grandma looks uncomfortable. "Maybe we should——"

Just then a man walks in and shuts the door behind him. He's older than Dad was. Maybe fifty. And he's wearing a pinstriped suit and running shoes. Something's weird about his hair. It hasn't got any grey in it. And it's really slick with gel.

"Mr. and Mrs. Matthews," he says, shaking their hands. "Hillary, nice to meet you," he says to me. "I'm Dr. Snead."

Why are these people calling me the wrong name? Why don't I have shoes?

The doctor sits down in a chair across from us and crosses one leg over the other. He folds his hands over his knee and presses the tips of his thumbs together. "I don't want to keep you too long, because I'm sure Hillary's tired and over-whelmed and ready to go home," he says.

What home? I think. *I'm not Hillary.*

"But it's important that we discuss some things first," Dr. Snead goes on. "Hillary has been through a lot, and she needs support right now."

"What exactly has happened?" Grandma says, taking my hand. "All we heard over the weekend was what was on the news, and then Tuesday the police called about my son and his family . . ."

"Are you ready to talk about what you've been through, Hillary?" Dr. Snead says.

I pull my hand away from Grandma's and tug my blanket tighter around my shoulders.

"Hillary hasn't been able to tell anyone what she's experienced yet." Dr. Snead sighs. "But I feel confident that she'll open up to us in time."

"Where did you find her?" Grandma says.

"Police found her in the woods near County Road 22 in Henderson," says Dr. Snead. "We think she must have been there on Sunday, because she was wearing a white dress."

"Why does that mean she was there since Sunday?" Grandpa asks.

"Well, her parents were Orthodox," Dr. Snead says. "It's traditional for them to wear white on Pascha, their version of Easter, which would have been this past Sunday."

"Always knew that cult would get Alex in trouble someday," Grandpa says, shaking his head. "I warned him over and over, but he never listened."

I barely hear Grandpa, I'm focusing so hard on Dr. Snead. How does he know that?

"You're not a religious man, Mr. Matthews?" Dr. Snead says.

"Used to be," says Grandpa. "Gladys and I went to church for a while, but it got me mad, listening to them telling me what to do and always asking for money. Just wanted to live my own life."

Dr. Snead nods. "It's been the downfall of Christians, especially the Orthodox. So critical of others, refusing to perform marriages, denying women's rights, condemning people who choose different paths . . . it's no wonder they made enemies."

"It's over now, though, right?" Grandma says worriedly. "Euph—I mean, Hillary will be safe with us?"

"Absolutely. That's what these changes are all about," says Dr. Snead. "Mass secularization has ended so much controversy and violence. It'll take a while for the government to change everything over, but these kinds of tragedies will cease to happen."

I'm so tired, I can't even figure out what they're saying. What's mass secularization? Is he saying it was my family's fault they got killed?

"So that's why the government has ordered churches to close?" Grandma asks. "Some people are saying the government's anti-Christian now."

"We aren't 'anti' anything," says Dr. Snead. "People will still be free to believe whatever they want. But religion will be a personal thing, different for everyone. It's when people try to force their beliefs on others that tragedy ensues. Just look at the Crusades."

But then why were policemen burning down St. John's? I think. If the government isn't anti-Christian, why are they making me change my name?

"The new system will be one of tolerance and acceptance," Dr. Snead goes on. "It's a terrible thing that so many were killed on Pascha. The individual lives are a great loss. But Orthodoxy itself? A union of religious extremists determined to condemn others? I think our nation will ultimately be better off without it. And Hillary, I know this is hard to hear right now, but I think you will ultimately be better off without it."

I can't think of anything to say to this person who's telling me that I'll be better off now that my family's dead and my whole world has ended. I just stare at my bare feet, wishing someone would give me some socks and shoes and let me be alone.

Dr. Snead gives his card to Grandma and Grandpa and has his secretary set up my first appointment with him. "See you in a week, Hillary," he says, patting me on the back. "Maybe we can talk a little more about what you've been through. It'll help you to open up to people."

I shrug my shoulders. I don't want to talk to anybody. And my name's not Hillary.

I follow Grandma and Grandpa out to the car. They are talking about my new room, how I'll have it all to myself, how I can decide how to decorate it. I don't want to cry in front of them, but I do. Their car smells weird, and it's too clean, and Kat's car seat isn't there.

It's a long ride to my new home.

December 12, 0000 ET

Mimi is standing in an alcove in the nonfiction section, running her finger along the book spines and muttering to herself.

"What are you doing?" I ask her.

She holds up one finger, and I wait until she comes to the end of a row. Then she sighs and writes something down on a slip of paper. "Shelf-reading," she says finally.

"What's that?"

"I'm checking that the books are all in order. By reading the numbers and letters written on their spines."

"Oh," I say. I step closer and look at the books more closely. "Why does '515.1244 BLA' come before '515.13 BLA'?" I ask. "Shouldn't the smaller number come first?"

"Well, since decimals are really fractions," Mimi says, "515.1244 is a smaller number."

"Oh. Oh, right." Math is not my thing.

"What grade are you in? Have you done decimals in school yet?" Mimi asks.

"Seventh grade. We've done them, I'm just not thinking straight these days."

"Me neither. That's why it makes my brain hurt to shelf-read."

I make a face. "I didn't think you'd have to do math to be a librarian." One more potential career scratched off my list.

"Unfortunately you have to do math for pretty much any job," says Mimi. "That's why they invented coffee."

"I don't really like coffee."

"I didn't when I was your age," says Mimi. "Then college happened."

I laugh. "My mom drank so much coffee. Like five or six cups a day. And she'd make one cup and forget it somewhere, so we were always finding half-cups of coffee on the bookshelf and in the bathroom . . ."

Mimi laughs too. "I may or may not have done that before." She shakes her head. "Gosh, Sunday mornings used to be so hard without coffee . . ." She trails off, and we both look at each other, our smiles fading.

I remember the book in my hand and hold it up. "I finished *Speak*."

Mimi takes the book from me and opens it up to smell the pages. That's kind of weird, but maybe not for a librarian. "What'd you think?"

"It was really good. It was more like real life than *The Giver*. I liked Melinda a lot. She reminded me of myself, I guess."

Mimi swishes out her skirt and sits down on the floor. I sit next to her, crisscross-applesauce. "We all go through hard stuff that we have to work to get past," she says quietly.

"Yeah. I always think about my mom and dad, and Kat, my sister. She was only six when she died."

"On Pascha?" Mimi whispers.

I nod. My heart starts to beat a little faster. I haven't talked to anybody about this since it happened. Can I trust her? Will she tell anyone?

"I always miss Alex," she says, barely loud enough for me to hear.

"Alex who?" I ask. Did she know my dad?

She twists the ring on her right hand. "My husband," she says. "I think about the night when he proposed . . . It was a Friday, so we couldn't even go anywhere good for dinner, but he made us peanut butter and jelly sandwiches, and we had a picnic on the floor of his apartment . . ." She trails off, smiling. I can tell it's the smile that means you might start crying any minute. Sweet but sad.

"Are you going to tell anyone?" she asks me.

I shake my head.

"Thank you," she says.

It must be pretty scary to tell a kid a secret that might get you killed. "How did you know that I was Orthodox?" I ask her.

"When you came in here before, with your parents, you used to have a three-bar cross around your neck," she says. "And once, a few months ago, I saw you crossing yourself when you walked across the center aisle of the children's section."

"Oh," I say, embarrassed. "I didn't know I did that."

"You don't usually do it," says Mimi. "I think you must have been thinking about church. Plus, the children's section is kind of laid out like a sanctuary, with that little stage-platform thing where the altar should be."

"I only knew you were Orthodox because you wear your ring on your right hand," I say. "And your name used to be Mary, but that didn't prove anything."

Mimi leans closer to me. "I'll tell you a bigger secret," she whispers. "I still am Orthodox. My name *is* Mary. And guess what? It always will be."

"They made me change mine to Hillary," I say. "I used to be Euphrosyne."

"After St. Euphrosynos the Cook?"

"Yeah. He was my patron saint."

"He still is your patron saint," Mimi whispers.

"What if he isn't, now that my name is different?"

"They can't change the name God gave you," Mimi says. "Besides . . . you want to know something really ironic?"

"What?"

"Hillary is an Orthodox name too," she says with a grin. She shakes her head. "And Mimi is short for Miriam, which is just another form of Mary. Somebody didn't do their research."

December 13, 0000 ET

It's cold outside, but they make us eat lunch on the picnic grounds anyway. All the kids have jackets on, and most of the girls are wearing those new scarves that are popular, the flannel ones that button together at the neck. I can see my breath streaming out of my nostrils, which reminds me of Kat, who always pretended she was a dragon. A beautiful dragon, though. One with purple scales.

Most people have finished eating, and they stand around in clumps, talking or bouncing in place to keep warm. I walk around the borders of the grounds, balancing on the wooden planks that keep the pebbles from spilling everywhere, just thinking about stuff and dreading seeing Dr. Snead tomorrow.

"What child is this, who, laid to rest, on Mary's lap is sleeping?"

I freeze, wobbling on the wooden plank. A girl leaning against the wall—the one named Boston—is singing to herself as she scrolls through her phone.

"Whom angels greet with anthems sweet, while shepherds watch are keeping?"

She's concentrating hard on the phone, her eyebrows furrowed. I don't think she even realizes she's singing.

"This, this is Christ the King, whom shepherds guard and angels sing; Haste, haste to bring Him laud, the babe, the son of Mary . . ."

Miss Linda, standing by the door on the other side of the picnic tables, straightens up and looks around, her eyes narrowed. I pray for Boston to stop singing.

She taps out a text message with her thumb and grins. "What child is this . . ." she starts again. And then, "Ow! Hillary, what is wrong with you? That hurt! I'm telling Miss Linda!"

I let the second handful of pebbles that I had picked up slide through my fingers.

"Miss Linda! Hillary Matthews just threw rocks at me!"

Miss Linda is coming towards us, dodging through a couple of the boys who are playing tag. "What? Hillary, is that true?"

"It was just a joke," I say.

"One of them hit me in the face," Boston says, rubbing a red spot on her cheek. "I wasn't even bothering her."

"Hillary, throwing rocks is unacceptable. You could really hurt someone."

I stare at the ground. "Sorry."

"I'm going to have to take you to the principal's office," Miss Linda says. "Come with me, young lady."

I follow her back to the gate with all the other kids watching me. I've never gotten in trouble before. I've never been sent to the principal's office before. Tears well up in my eyes.

They're going to tell Dr. Snead.

December 14, 0000 ET

"So. Not such a good week for you, hmm?"

They told him.

I shrug, and Dr. Snead goes on looking through my file. "Still got those A-plus grades, though. Even on your math quiz! Good job." He shuffles the papers and puts them away.

Then he leans forward so his elbows rest on his knees. He stares at me through his reading glasses. "So," he says. "Let's talk about how you're feeling."

Let's not, I think. "I don't know," I say out loud.

"You have a very expressive face, Hillary. It's always easy to tell when you're angry."

"I'm not angry."

He shakes his head. "You don't have to pretend for me. You can be honest. What's bothering you?"

"I don't know."

A muscle tightens in his jaw. It really annoys him when I say that. He's easy for me to read, too.

"Why did you throw the rocks at Boston, Hillary?" he asks me.

I stare at my hands. Then I realize I'm pulling at my fingers again, and I tuck them under my legs.

"Did she say something hurtful?" he asks. "Something about your past?"

"No."

"Something must have bothered you. I've never known you to hurt anyone before."

One of the most irritating things about Dr. Snead is that he talks like he knows you really well. Like he's your best friend, only a lot smarter than you, and you can't leave his office.

"I don't know."

Dr. Snead sighs. He sits back in his chair and pats his gelled hair absentmindedly. It makes a sound like leaves crunching. For a minute or two we sit silently, listening to the white-noise machine hum. It's another thing he does, trying to make me feel uncomfortable so that I'll say something. But I know better. I just let my brain wander until he's ready to ask me more questions.

"I imagine this is a difficult time of year for you," he says finally. When I don't say anything, he goes on. "The holidays are all about family and giving, and it's very natural for you to struggle during this season. Especially since it's the first one you've gone through since your parents passed."

I will not get upset. I will not.

"It is even natural," he says softly, "for you to experience some anger. Towards your parents. Your grandparents. Towards Orthodoxy."

"I'm not angry," I say.

Dr. Snead acts like he didn't hear me. "When I was a little boy," he goes on, "I believed in Santa Claus for a long time. Longer than most children. Winter Holiday, or Christmas, as we used to call it, was my favorite holiday, because of the magic and mystery. And then one year, I caught my parents filling my stockings. I was very angry. Angry like you are now."

"I'm not angry," I say again.

"Because I thought they had been lying to me," he says. "I thought it was all fake. The magic was gone."

I can't help but think about my empty shoes by the door on St. Nicholas Day.

"But you know what?" Dr. Snead says. "I came to realize

that the real magic was in my family and the things that we celebrated together. The game of Santa Claus was just a way that my parents showed me their love.

"Your parents' traditions—Orthodoxy, the Nativity, Santa Claus—all of those things were ways to celebrate together. They weren't what made the holidays magical. It was time with your family that was the real magic."

What he's saying sounds almost right. I'm so confused.

"You don't have to stay angry, Hillary," says Dr. Snead. "You know now that your parents weren't perfect. They taught you wrongly. But the important thing is not their worldviews, but their love for you. You can disagree with them and still respect their memory."

But I want it to be real, I think. *I want the real magic, I want it to mean something.*

"What are your plans for this Winter Holiday?" he asks.

I shrug. "I think we're just staying home. Uncle Robert and Aunt Cindy might come over. We're putting up Grandma's tree on Saturday."

Dr. Snead writes something down on a sticky note. "Your Uncle Robert—that's your dad's brother?"

"Yeah."

"And his daughter was the one who was staying with your family on Pascha?"

"Yeah." Olivia.

"But they weren't Orthodox?"

"No, they didn't go to church, but sometimes Olivia came with us."

"And you haven't seen them since Olivia died," Dr. Snead says.

"No." They live half an hour from Grandma and Grandpa, but they've never visited. Probably so they wouldn't have to see me. There were two beds in Kat's and my bedroom, and two girls. No one came looking for me under Mom and Dad's bed because no one knew there were three kids in the house.

"Are you nervous about seeing them again?" Dr. Snead asks.

"Yeah," I say.

"Maybe next week we can talk a little about that," he says. "You remind me, okay?"

"Okay."

He gets up and opens the door for me. We walk down the hallway and out to the waiting room, where Grandma is sitting and looking at pie recipes in a magazine.

"Did you have a good session?" she asks cheerfully.

"Great," says Dr. Snead, patting me on the shoulder.

I shrug.

"We've got to stop and get some Holiday cards on the way home," Grandma says. "Do you want to get a frozen pizza for dinner?"

"Mmm, pizza," says Dr. Snead. "I'm jealous!"

They laugh and chit-chat for a few minutes while Grandma gathers up her purse and things. Then Dr. Snead goes back into the office, and Grandma and I leave.

The air is cold and crisp outside the claustrophobic waiting room. I take a deep breath and then shiver. In the growing darkness the Holiday decorations are starting to twinkle on every telephone pole. There are holiday trees, snowflakes, and reindeer. And on one pole, at the corner of the street, a star. A song floats into my head, a memory of Mom's voice and mine blending together.

Today the Virgin gives birth to the Transcendent One,

And the earth offers a cave to the Unapproachable One!

Angels, with shepherds, glorify Him! The wise men journey with the star!

Since for our sake the Eternal God . . .

The voices grow soft with wonder.

. . . is born as a little child.

I stand still by the car, barely breathing, looking at the real stars appearing in the dark blue night above me.

If it's all a lie, why are they having such a hard time making me forget?

December 15, 0000 ET — 8:13 pm

After I do my math homework, I go up to my room and lie on my bed so I can stop being angry about circumferences and surface areas. My clock ticks loudly.

Having a clock is better than having a psychiatrist. At least a psychiatrist like Dr. Snead. Maybe there are good psychiatrists out there too, but I really just like my clock, because it doesn't ask me hard questions or try to get me to talk. It just ticks calmly. It never gets upset like Grandma or sneaky like Miss Linda.

I decide that if I have my own house someday, I'm going to put clocks in every room so that I'll have someone nice to talk to everywhere I go. I'll have big bookshelves filled with only my favorite books. The only people that I'll let come to visit me will be Mimi and Grandma. And in my house you will be able to say whatever words you want, like "Christmas" and "God," and no one will get you in trouble.

And there will be no math.

December 16, 0000 ET — 3:47 am

"Hillary! Wake up, Hillie-billie." Someone is shaking me by my shoulders. Someone who smells like flannel and Old Spice. Grandpa. What's going on? It's dark. I'm in the middle of saying something, but I can't remember what.

"You been talking in your sleep again," Grandpa says. "Woke up your grandmother."

"What time is it?" I ask thickly.

"About four in the morning," he says. "Did you have a nightmare?"

"I don't think so." I still feel confused.

"You were saying something about cats. Try and sleep quietly. Your grandmother has insomnia."

I hear him trudging out of my room and shutting my

door. He's always grumpy when he's sleepy.

Cats? That doesn't sound right. I stare at the dark ceiling. I need to go to the bathroom, but my blankets are warm and I don't want to get out of bed. Maybe I can fall back asleep and wait until morning.

"Kat, not cat," I say to myself.

And then I remember.

Kat is counting. I'm looking for a hiding place. But the trees around me are scrawny and far apart. I'm running out of time. Where can I hide?

I run farther from her, deeper into the forest, still looking. I know these woods. I've been here before. There's the creek. The fallen log. The dead tree with a hole inside it. It's a little hole, only big enough for a raccoon or a dog Hershey's size. But I seem to shrink as I run forward, and suddenly I'm inside.

"Peaches, pumpkin, apple pie, if you're not ready, holler 'aye!'" Kat's voice sounds faint.

The hollow in the tree is so dark and I am so small that she'll never find me. I push my way through the dead leaves and dirt, trying to get away from the opening. Then I see a light at the other end. What is that?

It's not daylight. It's whiter, more like starlight.

I walk toward it. How big is this tree? Or am I really small?

I clench the sheets of my bed in my fists. I want to call Grandpa back into the room, even if he is grumpy.

It's a man's face. A giant. His eyes are open, but staring upward. He looms above me, sitting propped against the wall of the tree, his legs outstretched and his hands folded gently over his stomach.

"Hello?" I say, but no noise comes out of my mouth.

His red slippers, as I walk past them, are as tall as I am. The folds of his crimson robe could swallow me. The blue crosses on his white stole are life-sized.

"Euphrosyne? Euphrosyne, where are you?"

The giant stirs at the sound of Kat's voice. His huge, white-bearded chin turns towards me. His face is kind, but so bright and scary that I stumble back, crying out. The giant laughs, stretching his arms out to catch me. His stole falls forward, and I see the bullet lodged in his chest, blood dripping from the wound.

The giant hands catch me and set me down gently.

"You found her!" says Kat, skipping up to us. She is wearing her favorite outfit—the princess skirt from her dress-up clothes, her pink cowgirl boots, and Dad's T-shirt with the mustache on it. She's got her backpack on, too.

"Katerina has a Christmas present for you," the giant says.

Kat takes off and unzips her backpack. "Hold out your hands!" she tells me.

I can't stop looking at the giant, but I do what she says.

Into the palms of my hands she places one, two, three small apples. She zips up her backpack and puts it back on, then leans to whisper in my ear.

"They're from the Cook," she says.

And then she skips off again.

"Kat!" I cry, finally finding my voice. "Wait, come back! Kat!"

December 16, 0000 ET — 4:28 pm

Mimi is tucked away in another nook of the nonfiction section, reshelving books from a cart. It took me a while to find her, but I had to talk to someone.

"Do you believe in miracles?" I ask her.

"Absolutely," she says.

"I mean, not just miracles in the Bible, but, like, nowadays."

"Absolutely," she repeats.

I stand beside her, looking at the titles of the books, trying to think what to say next. *The Brontë Sisters. Collected works of Charlotte Brontë. Gondal.*

"Have you ever seen one happen?" I ask her.

She peels the sticker off the spine of a book on the cart and replaces it with another, then shelves it. "No," she says. "Not that I know of, anyway. But I'm not very holy." She smiles.

"But I'm not holy either."

Mimi pauses in the middle of peeling a sticker off another book. "Have you seen a miracle?"

I nod.

For a few minutes she doesn't say anything. I keep waiting for her to ask me what it was. Then she says, "I think you need to see somebody."

"I'm not crazy," I say.

"No, no. Not a doctor. Well, not that kind of doctor."

I look at her suspiciously. Maybe I shouldn't have told her anything.

It seems like she's trying to decide something. "How old are you?" she asks.

"Twelve," I say. "Almost thirteen."

Mimi leans on the cart and sighs. "I don't know what I should do," she murmurs to herself.

"What are you talking about?"

She picks up a book and turns it over in her hands. "Euphrosyne," she says. "Do you know what kind of world we live in?"

That's a weird question. "I guess."

Mimi lowers her voice. "You are twelve years old," she says. "And you've seen things that twelve-year-olds aren't supposed to see. You're having to make decisions that twelve-year-olds aren't supposed to make. Are you aware——" Her voice gets even quieter. "——that people are watching?"

I think of Dr. Snead and Miss Linda, and I nod.

"Do you know what will happen if you get caught?"

"What?" I whisper.

"I have no idea," she whispers back. "But my husband is dead."

"My family is dead."

"Are you old enough to decide? Or should you be kept safe?" Mimi seems to be talking to herself now.

She's about to tell me something. Something important. Something that maybe I don't want to know. It's not too late. I can still go back to Grandma in the romance section, still go be a little kid and be safe. Let grownups worry about the scary stuff.

I think of the dream, and of the giant and Kat. And I want to know.

"Please tell me," I say.

Mimi crosses herself. I look around, frightened that somebody might have seen. There's no one near. "There's a used bookstore on the corner of Eighth Street and First Avenue downtown," she says. "The owner can help you."

A bookstore? How does that help? "Who is he?" I ask.

"Just go there, if you can, and ask to see a world atlas."

"A map book?"

Mimi nods. "He'll ask you what country you're interested in. And you tell him Sinai."

"That's not a country," I say. "Isn't that where Moses was when he got the Ten Commandments?"

She puts a finger to her lips, and I realize that my voice has gotten too loud.

"Sorry," I whisper. "But why should I say that?"

"Because no one would say that if they were just a regular person looking for an atlas. It's a secret password."

I nod. "And then what will happen?"

"I don't know," says Mimi. "He'll help you however he can. You can trust him completely. Just don't tell anyone."

"I won't."

She goes back to changing stickers and shelving. Her eyebrows are furrowed, and she looks worried. Maybe she thinks I'll give away the secret. I try to come up with a way to convince her I won't.

"Would you hand me that book?" she says, pointing to

the cart with her right hand while marking a spot on the shelf with her left.

I grab the book and start to hand it to her, then freeze, looking at the cover. It's an old Bible. The numbers on the new sticker match the numbers on the shelf, but the books on the shelf are all titled things like *Collected Works of John Donne* and *Metaphysical Poets* and *Sonnets of the Seventeenth Century*.

"Sometimes someone shelves a book in the wrong place," Mimi says, taking the Bible from my hands and sliding it in with the other volumes. "And then it's almost impossible to find again."

I scan the other books on her cart. Some of them are normal. But no, there is *Lives of the Saints* and *The Way of the Pilgrim*. "You're gonna get caught," I whisper.

Mimi nods. "Eventually. It'll take them forever to find all of these, though. And in the meantime, people will run across them and maybe read them. I'm figuring out a way to make them searchable, too. They've got fake names in the system, and once I give them all a tag subject, you'll be able to find them."

I don't really understand, but it sounds risky. *Please don't let her get caught*, I think. *She's the only friend I have.*

December 17, 0000 ET

"I like this fake tree so much better than the real ones," Grandma says to Grandpa. "It's so much cleaner. When the boys were little and we had the real trees, I was always having to vacuum up all those pine needles."

"Mmm-hmm," Grandpa says. He's drinking a beer and watching a football game on TV. I don't think he's paying much attention to either of us. He was supposed to be helping us put up the tree by now, but the game went into overtime.

I hate football. Dad used to watch it sometimes and tell us there were just ten minutes left in the game, and then he wouldn't play with us for another hour, because apparently they only count the time when the guys are running around and throwing the ball, not measuring things or arguing with each other or watching playbacks to see whether or not someone's foot went over the white line. Sports are only fun when grownups aren't involved.

Grandma and I sit on the living room floor and work on the tree. We've got the plastic trunk part up and all the fake branches separated into piles, and Grandma's twisting them in place while I fluff them up and try to make them look less pathetic. I think it must be a pretty old tree, because the box it came out of is dusty and torn, and some of the papery pine needles are missing from the branches. They must have bought it right after Dad went to college.

"Oh, this one needs some extra attention, Hillary," Grandma says, picking up a smaller branch that goes near the top. It's only got a few pine needles left on it, and they're all sticking out in different directions.

This is depressing. I want a real tree, one that smells good and is a little crooked and leaves sap on your hands when you're dragging it in from the car. I want Mom and Dad arguing about whether it's leaning or not and Kat and me arguing about who gets to put on the first ornament. I even want Hershey sneak-eating fallen pine needles and then throwing up on the rug.

The TV roars, and Grandpa says a bad word and shakes his head. "That's it," he says, taking a gulp of his beer. "It's over. No way they can come back from that."

"The game's over?" I ask.

"No, forty more seconds," Grandpa says without taking his eyes off the screen.

Who knows how long that will take. Grandma and I finish setting the tree up and then stand back to look at our work.

"It's great!" Grandma says.

"Yeah!" I say. Nope. It's pathetic. Maybe it'll look better with some decorations on it. "Are the lights in here?" I say, poking at one of the other dusty boxes that she dragged out from the closet under the stairs.

"I'm not sure," Grandma says. "All of the Christmas—I mean, Holiday—stuff is mixed up in there. We'll just have to go through it."

The lights are in the first box, completely tangled up. There are also bags of mismatched ornaments, half-burnt candles, old candy canes, and a teapot that looks like a ginger-bread house. And a bunch of tinsel at the bottom. Grandma and I pull everything out, and she starts to work on the knot of Christmas lights.

I open the second box. There are some stockings, one with Dad's name embroidered on it. I run my fingers over the letters. I wonder what's happened to my stocking. And everything else in my old house. Under the stockings are a stuffed Santa and Mrs. Claus, which are kind of creepy looking, since their stitched-on eyebrows are furrowed, and at the bottom is something wooden and pointy. "What's this?" I ask, lifting it out. It's heavy, and as I set it down, several small bundles of newspaper and tissue roll out onto the carpet.

Grandma's busy fighting the string of lights. "What's what, honey?" she asks.

"This wooden thing." I unwrap one of the little bundles. Inside is a porcelain figure of a bearded man, wearing a purple robe and carrying a golden box.

Grandma looks up. "Oh, Richard, I forgot about that. We'll have to get rid of it."

"What?" says Grandpa.

"The Nativity set," she says, glancing at him sideways as though she's afraid she might get in trouble.

"Oh that," Grandpa grunts. "Yeah, better go do that now."

He actually gets out of his recliner, even with just a few seconds left in the game, scoops the fallen bundles back into the wooden stable, and heaves it up under one arm. I hear some of the fragile wood crackle under the pressure. He holds out his hand for me to give him the Wise Man.

I hand it to him slowly, and he tosses it in with a *clink*. Then he trudges outside to drop the whole thing in the garbage. I can hear the crash of breaking china from inside the house. I wince, remembering the sound of the windows shattering on Pascha.

"You okay, Hillie-billie?" Grandma says softly.

"I don't know," I say.

She loops the first untangled string of lights in a circle over her arm. "It does seem like a shame," she says.

When Grandpa comes in we're all quiet, except for the football announcers on the TV, saying how this is the most critical game of the season and how nobody could have predicted that score. Grandpa's mad because he didn't see the ending, Grandma's busy putting up the lights, and I'm thinking about Mimi saving all those books and the little people lying in the garbage outside.

That night I sneak outside when Grandma and Grandpa are asleep and dig through the trash can. It was empty before Grandpa threw the Nativity set away, so I'm afraid to take away too much. They'd notice. But I take the Baby Jesus in the manger, and the Theotokos, and an angel with a broken wing. I want to get Joseph, but he fell out of his wrappings and is in three pieces, and I can't even find his head. So I put the cold figures in my jacket pocket and slip back inside. I hide them in the back of my desk drawer, behind the copy of *Number the Stars* that Mimi gave me to read. For some reason it's easier for me to fall asleep knowing that they're safe.

December 20, 0000 ET

"You all look so nice in your holiday clothes!" Miss Linda says, pressing her hands together. "Now I know you're all excited because of our party, but we have just a few things to do today! So sit down at your desks and try to stay focused!"

I can actually hear the exclamation points in her voice. Nobody looks that excited. A couple of girls are secretly looking at their phones.

Two people have their geography presentations in front of the class before we can eat the food we brought from home. The first boy, Austin, does his on Russia. It's not very creative. Most of his posterboard is taken up by a huge printout of the Russian flag, which looks fuzzy and has the Shutterstock logo running across it horizontally. I don't think he spent very much time on his speech, either, because he just read a bunch of facts off the back of an old math quiz. When he asks if anybody has questions, nobody raises their hands because none of them really care about Russia and they all hope that he'll sit down and stop talking.

I feel kind of bad for him, so I raise my hand.

"Yeah, you, umm . . ." he says, like he's trying to remember my name.

"What made you choose Russia as your country?" I ask.

"Oh, my dad's always saying we should just nuke them," says Austin.

Which is why I usually don't talk to boys.

The next presentation goes better. It's Boston, the girl I threw rocks at. You're welcome, Boston. She does her presentation on England. She's wearing a headband with the Union Jack on it, and a sweater with the TARDIS printed across the front, and at the top of her poster are the words "Keep calm and drink tea." Her picture of King William looks like she clipped it out of a tabloid magazine, but at least she has some facts I didn't know, and she shows us a photo of herself riding a double-decker bus. Some other people ask questions this time, and I don't have to embarrass myself.

The Winter Holiday party is okay. I sit with two girls named Hamilton and Sasha who are best friends and who don't mind if I sometimes hang around them. Everybody eats the frosted sugar cookies that I asked Grandma to get at the bakery. They don't get taken quite as fast as the brownies that Gates's mom sent, but they beat the Chex Mix and Rice Krispy treats, and I'm way better off than the kid who brought baby carrots and celery. So it's all good. I've made it through half the year. I can do this.

And tomorrow Grandma will take me Christmas shopping. Holiday shopping. At the bookstore downtown, the one Mimi told me about. I hope they have prairie romance novels.

THREE

December 21, 0000 ET

"Are you sure you don't want to go to Walmart or something, honey?" Grandma asks. We're standing outside the little shop and looking at the dusty books in the window. Most of them are tattered or bent. "Your grandpa doesn't like books that much. You could get him some fishing stuff. Or an Alabama mug, or something."

"I have to look in here," I tell Grandma. "And I have to buy you a present, too. You like books."

"That's true," Grandma says. She's being nice. She likes *new* books.

"I need to go alone so you won't see," I say. "Can I have my money?"

She takes out the ten-dollar bill I got for raking the front yard. "Are you sure you'll be okay in there?"

"Yeah, I'm sure."

"Okay, well, I'll get some coffee in that Starbucks over there and read my book until you're done." Grandma gives me a hug and then heads off.

As soon as she's gone, I hurry in. I can't take too long without her getting worried.

A bell on the door clangs as I open it. The shop smells

like old books and tea—a dusty, ticklish smell that I like right away. There are bookshelves taller than me in the center of the shop, and bookshelves lining the walls, and a glass counter displaying some books that look very old. Behind the counter is a doorway leading into the back, where I can see more books and a faded yellow couch with some of the stuffing coming out of it.

"I'll be right with you," comes a deep voice from the back.

I'm suddenly really scared. What am I doing here? I could get in so much trouble. I step forward to the counter, clutching my ten-dollar bill tightly.

An old man comes out from the back, carrying an armful of books with him. At least, I think he's old, because his hair and beard are mostly silver, except for a dark streak that runs down from his chin. But the hands gripping the books are huge, and there's something powerful in his walk and the way he stands. Maybe he's not so old after all.

"What can I help you with?" says the man as he sets the books on the counter.

"I need an atlas," I say nervously.

The man is silent for a moment, studying me. "Are your parents with you?" he finally asks quietly.

"They died," I say. "My grandma is next door getting coffee."

He doesn't react at all to the news that they're dead, just looks at me. His dark eyes don't blink, and I can't see his expression behind his beard. I have no idea what he's thinking. Or what I should do.

"I really need an atlas," I whisper.

"What country are you interested in?"

"Sinai," I say.

He nods. "I think I have an atlas in the back that might interest you," he says. "Do you have time to come take a look?"

"Yes sir."

"Come around the counter and I'll show you."

I walk around the glass case and follow him into the back of the shop. It's a small room, with the beat-up couch and piles of books and a desk with an old computer and a microwave. There's a mini-fridge in the corner and some pillows and blankets. I wonder if he lives here. It's cold, even though there's a space heater plugged in by the desk.

The man goes to the desk and opens the drawer. He takes out a large book, the kind that people put on coffee tables, and sets it on the desk. The cover is a photograph of a mountain, and the title is *Sinai*. Is he confused? Does he think I really want a book about Sinai?

"Is this what you're looking for?" he says, opening the book.

I come forward so I can see. Someone has cut a large square out of the middle of the book's pages. Inside rests an icon of Christ.

"Yes," I say.

The man steps back a little from the desk, crossing himself and bowing twice, then kisses the icon gently and crosses himself and bows once more.

It has been so long since I have done this. I pinch the first three fingers of my right hand together and draw an invisible line from my forehead to my stomach, then from my right shoulder to my left. I bend forward and touch my fingers to the dusty tile. My ponytail is longer than it used to be. It flops in front of my face when I bow a second time, and I have to brush it back. I kiss the icon and cross myself and bow again. I can feel both sets of eyes on me—the man's and Christ's.

"I'm Father Innocent," says the man. "What is your name?"

Father Innocent? The priest Mr. Liakos was taking me to see? I feel even more nervous. I've never talked to a priest by myself before, even though I grew up Orthodox. I was always too shy.

"I'm Hi—I mean, I'm Euphrosyne," I say. "Euphrosyne Matthews. My mom was Nicole and my dad was Alexander. We used to go to St. John's."

The priest nods. "I remember them," he says. "I think I remember seeing you and . . . do you have a sister?"

"She's gone," I say. The back of my throat hurts, and I swallow.

Father Innocent bows his head. "I'm very sorry."

"Mr. Liakos was taking me to see you," I say. "He thought you might still be alive."

"Reader Mark?" he asks, looking up quickly. "You know what happened to him?"

"He died, too," I say. "Some men stopped us on the road, and they killed him. I ran away."

This is the first time I have told anybody about what happened. They asked me over and over at the police station, at Dr. Snead's office, and at Grandma and Grandpa's house.

Father Innocent sinks into the chair by the desk and puts his head in his hands. "How am I going to tell Daniel?" he says to himself.

"But something happened when they tried to shoot me," I go on. My heart's beating fast, just remembering running through the woods, searching for a place to hide. "I think it was a miracle. That's why Mimi—I mean Mary—told me I should come talk to you."

"What happened?" asks the priest.

"A man was chasing me. And I was holding the icon Mom gave me—"

"Which icon?"

"St. Nicholas. And I turned around because I heard him coming, and he shot him."

Father Innocent blinks. "Who shot whom?"

"The man who was chasing me shot St. Nicholas," I say. "I mean, he was shooting at me, but I was holding up the icon, and the bullet went into St. Nicholas instead of me. It didn't even go through the wood. It just got stuck in his chest. And when I pulled it out . . ." I pause. "When I pulled it out it started bleeding."

"Where is the icon now?" Father Innocent asks.

He seems so calm. Did he even hear me? "I hid it in the woods. In a hollow tree," I say. "But I had a dream a few nights ago, and I think I have to go back and get it—"

The jingle of bells interrupts me. "Hillary?" comes Grandma's voice from the front.

Father Innocent and I both jump.

"I'm back here, just a second," I call.

The priest closes the *Sinai* book quickly and stands up. "I'll get in touch with you soon. Through Mary," he says in a low voice. "In the meantime, don't do anything risky."

I nod.

"Hillary, where are you? We're going to be late for your appointment with Dr. Snead."

"I said just a second," I say. There's a pile of paperback romances by the door. I grab a less beat-up copy and hurry out.

Father Innocent follows me. "I hope that's what you were looking for," he says, punching some buttons on the cash register.

"Yes, F—I mean, yes sir. How much is it?"

Grandma comes to stand next to me, sipping at her coffee and looking at the old books in the glass case. She doesn't have any idea what's going on.

"Grandma, don't look at your present!" I say.

"The paperbacks are a dollar each," says the priest.

I hand him my ten-dollar bill, and he gives me change and a paper bag for the book. "Thanks," I say. "Happy Holidays."

"Merry Christmas," he says quietly.

Grandma looks up, narrowing her eyes like he said a bad word. "Come on, it's time to go," she says, taking me by the hand and pulling me out of the shop.

She shakes her head as we walk to the car. "Poor man,"

she says. "It's us older folks who have such a hard time adjusting to change."

In the car ride to Dr. Snead's office, I sit and pretend to read *Number the Stars* while I think about what just happened. A priest is alive. The same priest Mr. Liakos wanted to go see. How did he escape? Does this mean Orthodoxy still exists? He said something about Daniel, Mr. Liakos's son. Is he still alive too? He was out of the country on Pascha. I can't remember where, somewhere in Europe, I think.

Something is bothering me. Something I don't want to bother me, something I try not to think about, but it keeps popping up in my head. It's so bad that I put the book down and start pulling at my fingers.

Why is Father Innocent alive?

I should not be thinking this.

Why did he get to live when my parents and Kat are dead? That's not fair. They were just normal people, and he was a priest. If anybody should have died, it should have been him.

I cringe at the idea. I can't believe I'm having these thoughts, but it's really bothering me. He was a priest. He was one of the most Orthodox people in the church. He was a leader. Why did he get to live when the people he was supposed to take care of died? It's not fair. It's not fair that my family is dead, but he's not.

Well, do you want him to be dead too? That doesn't solve anything, part of me says. I don't know how to answer. It wouldn't make anything better, and it's a terrible thought to have, but it doesn't seem fair the way it is.

You're alive too. And you were Orthodox, but Olivia wasn't. Shouldn't she be alive instead of you? How is it any different?

I feel the wave of guilt that I always get when I think about Olivia. I don't think about her enough. I only have so much sadness in me, and most of it is used up on Mom and Dad and Kat. But Olivia was nice. She was a good cousin. She always let me ride her bike when we went over to her house, and sometimes she let me take pictures with her expensive camera that still used real film.

Father Innocent doesn't deserve to be alive when my parents are dead, and I don't deserve to be alive when Olivia's dead. Nothing is fair. It all seems random, who had to die and who got to live. Like God isn't even in control. He asks us to do all these things, and then He doesn't take care of us.

But He did take care of you.

I remember the gunshot, falling backwards, the bullet in the icon.

But why me? Why not them?

I sit silently, staring at the cover of my book. I can't figure it out. I saw a miracle. I actually saw it. The icon stopped the bullet, and St. Nicholas started bleeding when I pulled it out. So God *could* stop people from dying.

That almost makes me mad. If God is in control, then He chose to let Mom and Dad and Kat and Mr. Liakos get killed. It's almost as bad as if He killed them. I can't stand that thought. But He saved me, so am I really allowed to be mad at Him? When I'm alive?

Either He's terrible or He's smarter than I am. Because I just don't understand. And it scares me to think this way. Everything used to be clear and simple before Pascha. You go to church, you do the right things, you're happy and safe. Now it's all messed up and complicated.

We're pulling into the parking lot of Dr. Snead's office, and I feel confused and mad. I don't want to talk to him. He doesn't know anything. It must be great to believe that being a nice person and just doing whatever you want will make you happy and safe. Has he ever been shot at? Has he ever been rescued by a God that let his parents die? We little human beings, we're not in control. Things happen to us, and maybe we deserve them, maybe we don't.

I've gotten myself all upset thinking about this stuff, and I've got tears in my eyes by the time we walk up the stairs to the office and sign in at the reception desk.

All this is so fake, I think, looking around at the plastic plants and uncomfortable chairs. Everything about this world is fake and watered down—the holidays, the people, the "just accept everybody" thing that Dr. Snead keeps telling me. How do they all live in this place and not go crazy? My grandparents, Miss Linda, the other kids in school? Do they really believe this is all there is?

Maybe I know better because of what I've been through. Or maybe I'm just crazy and trying to make it all mean something.

"Hillary?" Dr. Snead's voice interrupts my thoughts. There he is, watching me through his thick-rimmed glasses, holding my file under one arm.

"I want to go home," I say.

"What?" Grandma says, surprised.

"I want to go home," I repeat.

"Hillary, why don't you come in for at least a few minutes, and we can talk about——"

"I don't want to talk about anything! None of you get it!" I stand up. I'm starting to cry now, and the other patient in the waiting room, a middle-aged lady with an expensive haircut, is pretending not to watch from behind her magazine.

"I know you feel this way now," Dr. Snead begins, but I interrupt him.

"You don't know anything about it," I sob. "Just leave me alone. I want to go home." I turn to head for the door, and Grandma grabs my arm. I yank it away and then start crying harder because it hurts.

"I want to go home," I cry, and I don't know whether I'm talking about Grandma's house, or my old house, or just some place somewhere where everything makes sense and someone can hug me. I want to talk to Mimi or Father Innocent and ask them why bad things happen.

"We're already here. You need to go in and talk to Dr. Snead," Grandma says.

I sit back down in the chair, covering my face with my hands and shaking.

"Come on, Hillary. You can do this. Talking about these difficult feelings will help," Dr. Snead says, laying a heavy hand on my shoulder.

I cry for a few more minutes, and finally they get me

to go back into his office. But by then I feel numb. I sit and listen to him talk about sharing feelings and different kinds of families and the spirit of the holidays, and I study the laces of his running shoes.

"Are you feeling any better?" he asks at the end of the session.

"I don't know," I say.

December 22, 0000 ET

When I wake up, I can tell something is different. My room is still dark, and it's cold. Really cold. There are flowers of frost on the corners of my window. But the thing that's different is the silence. It's a muffled silence, like the house is wrapped in a quilt.

I sit up, pulling the blanket around my shoulders and swinging my legs off the bed. "Aghh," I groan. The hardwood floor is freezing. I shuffle to the window and look out.

The orange light from the streetlamp gleams faintly on a blanket of snow. There are no footprints anywhere, no people or animals in sight, just the snow and the streetlight and the dark hedges under my window.

I hurry to my dresser and put on some jeans and a long-sleeved shirt and hoodie. I grab socks and sneakers from my closet and take them with me, tiptoeing out into the hall, down the stairs, through the living room, and to the front door. In the dark I put on one of the socks inside-out, but I don't care. I just want to get out in the snow.

My footprints are the first to break through the thin crust of powder and ice. I crunch across the yard, taking deep, cold breaths. Everyone else in the neighborhood is asleep. It's a magical feeling.

I look back at the house. Grandma and Grandpa's window is dark, and the curtains are closed. Someone forgot to turn the tree lights off, though. They twinkle red, green, blue, and yellow through the living room blinds.

No one's watching me.

I dance around a little, twirling and leaping, the ice squeaking under my feet. Soon my socks are wet and I'm breathing hard, but I don't care. I twirl again and slip and fall. I lie back and make a snow angel.

"I wish Kat were here," I whisper to myself.

She loved snow. Here in Alabama you only get it once or twice a year, if you're lucky. Kat always wanted it to snow on Christmas, but it never did.

The melting ice starts to seep into my jeans, and I stand up, wiping off my seat. Thinking about Kat makes all my worries from yesterday return. I look up at the dark sky without meaning to, like I'm going to see God up there or something.

No God in sight, but a few stars blink back at me.

For some reason it's easier to believe in God when you're standing alone in the snow on a cold morning and looking at the stars.

"This is real," I say. My voice sounds weird. "This is real," I repeat.

I want to do something. This never happens any more. I never have time when I'm not being watched. I could run away. Maybe find the tree where I hid the St. Nicholas icon and get it back. I could take some food from the kitchen, and an extra jacket, and Grandpa's hat with the earflaps . . .

But I can't drive. And I don't even know exactly where the woods are. Somewhere on County Road 22, somewhere between a McDonald's and Father Innocent's trailer. That could be a big area, though.

A square of yellow light falls across the snow in front of me, and I turn around. Grandma and Grandpa's bedside lamp is on, glowing through the closed curtains.

They would find me before I got anywhere near the woods. And probably ask me where I was going, and tell on me to Dr. Snead, and then everyone would watch me even more closely than before.

I take a last breath of frosty air and slip back inside. It's no use pretending I wasn't out—my footprints are all over the yard, and my shoes and socks are wet. I strip them off and leave them by the door to dry. Grandma won't like that, but she'd be more upset if I tracked water all over the house.

The light is still on under their doorway when I tiptoe by. There's no noise from inside. Maybe Grandma can't sleep and is reading again. The clock in the living room only says 4:02 am. I have time to change into my fuzzy pajama pants and snuggle under the covers until I fall back to sleep.

December 24, 0000 ET

The snow is all melted when Uncle Robert and Aunt Cindy pull up in their new blue car.

"Hey! There they are!" Grandpa says, throwing his arms up and going forward to get hugs. "Nice car, Robert, nice car! What happened to the van?"

Uncle Robert slams his door shut and gives Grandpa a quick hug before going to pop open the trunk. "We decided to downsize. Get something with more style, now that . . . space isn't an issue."

This is not going to be a fun weekend.

Aunt Cindy gets out and fixes her skirt and overcoat. She looks thinner than the last time I saw her. And she's wearing more makeup. She hugs Grandma and Grandpa, and gives me a nod.

Aunt Cindy used to make us macaroni and cheese. She'd give me a big hug every time Kat and I came over.

I stand awkwardly on the doorstep, pulling my fingers.

"Well come on in!" Grandma says, patting Aunt Cindy's overcoat. "We've got the guest bedroom made up for you two, so you can put your stuff up there, and then relax a little. I know Richard has that game he wants to watch, and Robert, you probably want to watch it too. Cindy, I don't remember how much you like football, but I told Hillary we'd make some sugar cookies, and we could use some help."

"Hillary?" Aunt Cindy says blankly.

Everybody looks at her.

"Hillary," Grandma repeats, laying a hand on my shoulder. I wish I could disappear.

"So that's what they're calling you now, huh?" Aunt Cindy says.

"Yeah," I say.

"That's nice," she says. She turns to Grandma. "Actually, I was planning on seeing if there's a QuikFit gym near you guys. I'm doing this program right now, and it's really important that I go every day."

"Cindy's lost a lot of weight since—recently," Uncle Robert says. "She keeps telling me I need to cut calories, but I'm too attached to my beer."

Grandpa laughs and opens the door for us all to go in. "Can't keep a man from his beer, Cindy," he says.

Aunt Cindy is already on her phone, looking for a gym. I think she was prettier before she lost weight. Now she seems grey and tired. Except for all the makeup.

Once we're inside, Uncle Robert and Grandpa turn on the TV, and Grandma and I go into the kitchen. Aunt Cindy disappears upstairs.

Grandma gets out the recipe and two of her silver mixing bowls, and I go to the pantry to grab the flour and sugar. I'm glad there's something I can do besides sit around and talk to Uncle Robert and Aunt Cindy.

"Do we need baking soda, or powder?" I ask, scanning the stained index card.

"Powder," says Grandma. "Do you want to mix the flour and stuff while I cream the butter and sugar?"

"Okay."

I measure everything out carefully and then stir it around with a fork, making swirls and patterns in the flour. Sometimes Mom used to bake the prosphora for church. She'd trace a cross in the flour with her finger before adding the warm water and yeast.

"We'll have to hurry and decorate these once they're cooled," Grandma says, smushing the butter and sugar with a potato masher. "Otherwise we won't have cookies to put out for Santa."

I pause in swirling the flour. "Santa Claus?"

"You have to leave milk and cookies for Santa Claus!" Grandma looks at me, surprised. "Or he might put coal in your stocking."

I didn't know we were doing the whole Santa Claus thing here. "Are we hanging up stockings?"

"Of course," Grandma says.

"But my stocking—" I think of my stocking, with the embroidered letters *Euphrosyne* all cramped together on the border. "I don't have it anymore."

"Why don't you look in the bag by the stairs?" Grandma says, smiling.

Did she have my stocking? Had she saved it somehow? I drop the fork and race to the stairs, almost running into Aunt Cindy as she comes down in expensive yoga pants and tennis shoes. "I'm off to the gym," she says, zipping up her jacket.

"Have fun," says Grandpa, taking a sip of beer.

There's a bag at the foot of the stairs with the words

Monograms, Etc. on it in pretty cursive letters. I reach inside and pull out a large stocking.

It's pink. With white polka-dots and a lime-green border. And *Hillary* embroidered at the top in a cutesy font. I'd love it if it were a beach towel. But I can't help thinking of my old, ugly red stocking with the strings unraveling at the toe and the picture of the Christmas tree peeling off. And my real name.

"Do you like it?" Grandma asks from the kitchen door, wiping her hands with a paper towel.

"Yeah," I say. "It's great. Is this my Winter Holiday present?"

"No, silly," Grandma says. "You'll get those tomorrow! Now hang up your stocking!"

"Where?" They don't have a fireplace.

"Alex and Robert always used to hang theirs up on the coat rack," says Grandma.

I go to the coat rack by the door and hang the stocking on one of the highest hooks. It's so new that it hangs stiffly, still stocking-shaped. My old one used to droop.

"Thanks, Grandma," I say, giving her a hug. It was a nice thing for her to do. I try to look happy.

December 25, 0000 ET

It smells like bacon.

That's why I wake up. I blink and look at my clock. 7:30. The latest I've ever slept on a Christmas morning. Kat always woke me up when it was still dark. We'd sneak into the dining room and get our stockings off the fireplace, then snuggle in my bed and pull out one thing at a time until we hit the bottom. The rule was no waking up Mom and Dad until after six.

The bacon smells good. I think there might be eggs, too. When I open my bedroom door and head for the stairway, I can hear sizzling and coffee percolating.

"Good morning, Hillie-billie," Grandpa says as I come into the kitchen. He's sitting on a stool at the island, watching Grandma make breakfast. "Want some coffee?"

I make a face. Then I remember Mimi said she eventually started liking it, and I say, "Well, maybe a little bit."

"No way, Joseph," says Grandpa. "Caffeine will stunt your growth.

"Don't you mean 'no way José'?" I ask.

"This is America," Grandpa grunts.

"Oh, that's mean, Richard," Grandma says. "Let her try a little, now that you've offered. I'll put a lot of milk and sugar in it. Hillary, have you looked in your stocking yet?"

"Oh yeah!" I say. I hurry into the living room and take my bulging stocking down. It's really heavy. I go back into the kitchen and sit next to Grandpa at the island.

"What'd you get?" he asks, holding out a mug for Grandma.

"I don't know yet," I say, peeking into the stocking.

"Well, go ahead and dump it all out and see."

"No, I've gotta do it one thing at a time." I pull out the first gift and lay it on the island. A pink metal water bottle with the initials *HM* on it. "Wow, this is nice," I say, feeling Grandma and Grandpa's eyes on me. "That'll be good for school!"

There are two silver headbands, a mini sketchpad, a barrette with a flower on it, four squiggly-shaped pencils, a pack of playing cards, and lots of chocolates wrapped in red and green foil. All good stuff, but it's kind of weird having to act so excited about each thing. And there's always that super awkward moment when you have to feel around to make sure you didn't miss anything, and it looks like you think you didn't get enough.

"Wow, that's great," I say, smiling at all the stuff and twisting my fingers under the counter. "I'm gonna go take it all up to my room."

I load the presents back in my stocking and head upstairs. The guest room door is closed now, and it was only cracked when I went down. I pause. I hear muffled sounds of somebody crying inside.

I go into my room and carefully shut the door behind me. I drop the stocking on my bed and open my desk drawer. In the back is the porcelain Theotokos from the manger scene. The folds of her gown and headscarf are cold and smooth under my fingers. I curl up under my quilt on my bed and stare at her face, trying not to think about anything, just looking.

It's not my fault.

It's not my fault.

Everything is so tangled and messed up and fake, and everyone's pretending. Why are we all acting like we're happy?

Mary's expression is so calm. My breathing slows a little as I study her eyes, and I realize I must have been clenching my jaw, because now I release it. I lie still and memorize every detail of her face.

Later Grandma calls me down to breakfast, and I find Aunt Cindy and Uncle Robert sitting at the island drinking coffee. I don't know where Grandpa is. Aunt Cindy's eyes look a little puffy, but she's already put her makeup on, so it isn't that obvious. Nobody's talking.

"There you are, Hillary," says Grandma. "We've got bacon and scrambled eggs, and I'm about to pull these orange rolls out of the oven. Grab yourself a plate. Cindy and Robert, you two better eat fast, 'cause I'm sure Hillary is ready to open some presents!" She gives me a big smile.

I don't really care, but I laugh to be polite.

It's terrible to be the only kid at Christmas. Maybe kids without brothers or sisters are used to it and it doesn't bother them. I feel awkward through the whole present-opening thing, like we're all doing this for my sake and I have to be happy or I'll disappoint everyone. Well, disappoint Grandma.

Uncle Robert and Grandpa look bored, and Aunt Cindy is sitting very still and staring at her hands. The grownups give each other a few things, and then I'm left opening presents by myself. Grandma got me a bunch of stuff.

"Whoa," I say, pausing as I tear snowman paper off a smaller box. "Is this a phone?"

"A smartphone!" Grandma says. "The man at the store told me it was the best kind! Did you know you can play music on that thing?"

"Wasn't this really expensive?" I ask, turning the box over and looking at the back.

"Don't you worry about that," Grandma says.

"Can we hurry this up a little?" Grandpa says, glancing at his watch. "There's that Winter Holiday game at ten."

I get a lot of nice clothes and stuff from Grandma and Grandpa. And a fifty-dollar Walmart gift card from Uncle Robert and Aunt Cindy. Wow. I feel bad because I didn't think about getting them anything. I could have at least drawn them a picture. Grandma makes a big deal about how much she likes the book I got her at Father Innocent's bookstore— *Heart of the Highwayman*, with a picture of a shirtless guy in a kilt staring off at a dark and stormy landscape—and Grandpa laughs and says "She's got me figured out pretty good!" when he opens the coffee mug that says *Grandfather knows best!*

We turn on the TV and catch the end of the Winter Holiday Special before the game comes on. It seems pretty good. I like the part with the ice skaters, even though they must be really cold in those costumes. The Santa Claus parade is good too. The singers are only okay. They keep singing songs that don't sound Christmas-y to me.

Just give me a night with you, babe
That's all I want this year
Just kisses by the fire
And a cup of Holiday cheer!
Oh! Love ya, Santa! Oh!

Really none of this feels like Christmas. I should be with Mom and Dad and Kat, dressed in red and waiting for the liturgy to start. Smelling the incense and listening to the bells. The "Winter Holiday" isn't all bad, it's just kind of flat. Like taking a drink of Coke and finding out that all the fizz is gone. It's still sweet, but it doesn't send shivers up your spine.

"Whoa, what does he think he's doing?" Uncle Robert interrupts my thoughts.

The singer on TV, a guy with a ponytail and a plaid shirt, has just started to sing *Silent Night*. The audience suddenly goes quiet. He's not even using his guitar, just singing into the microphone.

"Fool's gonna get himself killed," Grandpa grunts.

"All is calm, all is bright, round yon Virgin Mother and Child. Holy Infant, so tender and mild. Sleep in heavenly peace . . ."

It's not an Orthodox carol, but the choir used to sing it after the liturgy on Christmas. And Mom would hum it when she was tucking us in on Christmas Eve.

"Sleep in heavenly peace."

The singer stops as two men in black suits walk onto the

stage. One of them says something we can't hear, and the singer nods. The other man grabs his arm to lead him off-stage, but before he can, the singer leans into the microphone.

"Christ is born, everybody," he says, giving a little wave goodbye.

"Glorify Him," I whisper automatically.

"What'd you say, Hillary?" Grandpa says sharply.

"Nothing."

Grandpa shakes his head at the screen. "Idiot. Some people just can't move on."

"I always liked that song," says Grandma to herself.

"Too sentimental," Uncle Robert says, settling into the couch as the opening music of the football game plays.

Aunt Cindy and I go upstairs as the others watch the game. I'm carrying a big armful of presents, and I have to go slow on the steps since I can't see my feet, and I get the feeling that she's annoyed at having to wait. As soon I'm out of her way she brushes past me and heads for the guest room.

"Hey, Aunt Cindy?" I say.

She pauses with her hand on the doorknob. "What?"

I don't know how to say it. I try to look at her face to see if she's mad, but she's just staring at the floor, waiting for me to say something.

"What?" she says again.

"I'm really sorry," I mumble. It sounds lame.

She gives a little snort. "What do you have to be sorry for? You're just a kid." She goes into the guest room and shuts the door.

Then why do you hate me now? I ask silently.

I go into my bedroom and lay my presents out on the floor, the way Kat and I used to do every Christmas. The phone is more expensive than anything Mom and Dad ever got me, but when I look at it my throat starts to hurt. I have no one to call.

I would trade it all just to talk to them again.

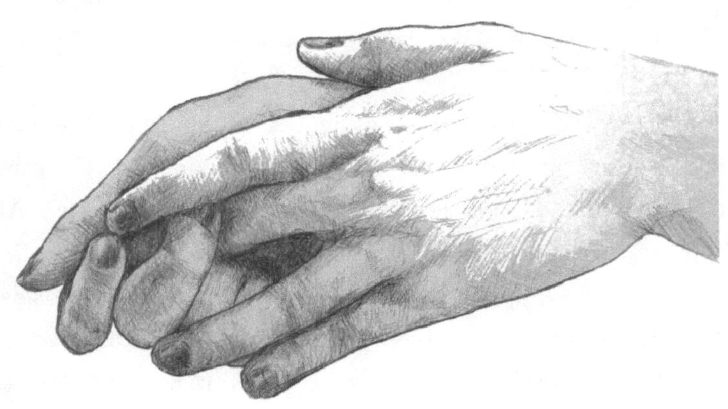

December 26, 0000 ET

The library is open from ten to five on Tuesday. Grandma seems happy to get out of the house for a while. I think when Grandpa's not at work, he gets on her nerves. She heads for the romance section, and I wander away to find Mimi.

I find her in the juvenile section, standing next to a big

man with pink skin and white hair. He kind of looks like our janitor at school, except better dressed, and he isn't smiling. He has one of the library carts with him and he's pulling books from the shelves.

"*Narnia,* obviously," he's saying. "*Elsie Dinsmoor.* Anything by Madeleine L'Engle. That one by Avi, *Cross of Lead* I think it's called. What's this? I'm not familiar with a lot of these. You'll have to use your discretion."

"We're not going to have much left," Mimi says, laughing uncomfortably. "We'll have to order some new juvenile fiction."

"I've got a catalogue coming out in January," the man says, pulling out *A Wrinkle in Time* and dropping it in the cart. It lands splayed open, but he doesn't bother to fix it. "All approved authors. You can fill in the gaps from there."

Mimi picks up *A Wrinkle in Time* and lays it on its side. "And are we just putting these on the twenty-five–cents shelf?"

"No, definitely not." The man looks at her in surprise. "The whole point is to stop exposing youth to these harmful ideas. Technically they should be shredded, but off the record, a lot of libraries are just tossing them. It's easier and faster."

"Got it," says Mimi.

The man tosses a few more books in the cart and then checks his watch. "I've got to be going. Last thing—for every book pulled, you need to print out the history of patrons who checked it out and send it to regional."

Mimi looks stunned. "There are a lot of kids . . ."

"I know, it's a ton of paperwork," the man sighs. "You only have to print out the first page of records, though. We're really not interested in anything going back more than two years."

"Well, that's a relief," Mimi says. But I can see that her knuckles are white from gripping the book cart.

"You can have someone else do it, if you want," the man says. "As long as it gets done. I'll be expecting a file from you in two weeks at the latest." He shakes her hand. "Happy Holidays."

I duck behind a bookshelf as he walks past. When I come out, Mimi is wiping her hand off on her skirt.

"Christ is born," she says to me quietly.

"Glorify Him," I answer. I take a folded piece of paper out of my pocket and give it to her.

"What's this?" she asks. She opens it up. "Whoa, is this for me?"

"Yeah," I say, a little embarrassed. I drew it with the set of colored pencils I got for Christmas.

"This is awesome!" Mimi laughs.

"See, that's you," I say, pointing at the librarian in the center of the page. She's wearing a flowery skirt and has a book in one hand and a sword in the other. There are lots of book characters behind her—a boy and a baby riding on a sled, a teenager with her arms wrapped around the trunk of an oak tree, four children with crowns on, a winged centaur, a girl with a basket, and many others.

"Man, you are such a good artist!" Mimi says, studying

all the details. She wraps an arm around me and gives me a hug. "Thank you, Euphrosyne," she whispers. "This makes my day a lot better."

I grin. I'm more proud of the picture than of the book I got Grandma or the mug I got Grandpa, even though it didn't cost me any money.

"I've got something for you too," Mimi says. "Here, come with me. I'll come back to this later." She gives the cart a little kick with her foot.

We walk back to the nonfiction section, past the bathrooms, and to a black door that says "Employees Only."

"Am I allowed in there?" I say as Mimi holds the door open for me.

"You're with me."

Inside is just a messy room with boxes of books, a refrigerator, and a dry-erase board. It reminds me of Father Innocent's room at the bookshop, but with the smell of Expo markers instead of tea. Mimi goes to a cabinet and takes something out. It's a fleece jacket, wrapped around something square and hard. An icon? No, a book. She hands it to me.

A Wrinkle in Time.

"Hey, isn't this the book that man put in the cart?" I ask, turning it over to look at the front cover.

"Yep. He wants me to get rid of all those," she says.

"Why?"

"They have stuff about Christianity in them," she says. "I should have seen it coming. They've already started curriculum changes in the schools. Libraries are next."

I open the book and flip through the pages. "Oh, hey, there's something inside here," I say, taking out an envelope. It has an *E* written on the back.

"That's for you from Father Innocent," Mimi says, whispering even though there's no one else in the room. "Read it someplace safe and then destroy it, if you can."

I tuck it back into the pages of the book. "Okay."

My jacket pocket vibrates, and I jump. "Oh, my Grandma's texting me," I say, taking it out. "I got a phone for Christmas."

You bout ready to go? says Grandma's text.

I type back, *Yeah just a minute.*

"Hey, can I have your phone number?" I ask Mimi.

"Um, let me think about that," she says. "I'll let you know the next time you come." She watches me put my phone in sleep mode and stow it in my pocket again. "Do your grandparents have your passcode?" she asks.

"Yeah, my grandpa set it for me," I say.

Mimi nods. "Be careful what you do on there then. Remember that people can see the messages you send and what you've been searching on the Internet."

I hadn't thought of that. "I will."

We walk back to the front, and Mimi waves goodbye to me. When I turn to look at her before Grandma and I walk out, I see her unfolding the picture I drew her again. She smiles, but when she closes her eyes and takes a deep breath, I wonder if she also might be about to cry.

IC
ON

December 27, 0000 ET

The letters are full of strange slashes and loops, and they're
hard for me to read. It's not cursive, just the way someone's
writing gets when they spend years taking notes. Mom's used
to look the same way.

Christ is Born!

*I have been thinking and praying a lot about your situa-
tion and the item you mentioned to me. There is a certain
extent to which I am responsible for you, and I do not
take that lightly. If you were younger I would advise you
to focus on school and remembering the things your parents taught you. I am still not sure I shouldn't do that.
But you are beginning to be old enough to make your own
choices, and I know there have been others like you who
have, with God's help, succeeded.*

*I give you my blessing to pursue this life and recov-
er the item we spoke of, but be sure you understand the
consequences. You know better than anyone what could
happen to you, what could be taken away from you. It
will be difficult.*

*If you decide you are not ready, I will try to take care
of the item myself. Please try to avoid doing or saying
anything that will endanger others. If you want to move
forward, my phone number is at the bottom.*

——*FR. INNOCENT MILANOVITCH*

I select the button to add a new contact on my phone and then type in the number. When I get to the space for a name, I pause. If Grandma or Grandpa look in here, I don't want anything that would make them suspicious. Finally I type in *Austin*, the name of that boy from school who gave the lousy Russia presentation. I don't know if I'm brave enough to write back or not. I'll think about it.

December 28, 0000 ET

"Have a seat, Hillary," says Dr. Snead. Something's different about him. His hair. It's usually slicked back with gel, but today it's dry and parted in the middle. I didn't know he had bangs.

"So how was your Winter Holiday?" he asks, crossing one knee over the other and flipping open a yellow notepad. He looks at me over his glasses.

"It was okay."

"Good, good. What did your family do?"

"Um. We had breakfast together. Uncle Robert and Aunt Cindy were there, and we did presents and stuff. And then they watched the football game."

"Sounds like a nice, relaxing day," says Dr. Snead, writing something down on the notepad. "Probably pretty different from what you're used to, though, huh?"

"I guess."

"I can imagine that Winter Holiday last year was a lot busier. Your family would go to church on Winter Holiday, right?"

I nod. I wish he would stop saying "Winter Holiday" instead of "Christmas."

"How did you handle the change in pace this year?" he asks. "Was it nice to be able to relax and celebrate the way you wanted?"

"I don't know."

"I'm sure you missed some aspects of Winter Holiday that you were used to," Dr. Snead goes on. "But did you start some new traditions?"

I'm getting annoyed. He keeps trying to make me say that I liked it better or something. "Maybe," I say. "It was nice to sleep in."

Dr. Snead looks pleased. He writes something down and underlines it. "I bet it was. You got to rest and enjoy the day. What other things would you like to make a part of your future Winter Holidays?"

I try to think of something. Not listening to my aunt cry because her kid is dead. Not opening presents alone with everybody watching me. "Maybe baking cookies with my Grandma," I say.

He writes it down, smiling.

"And seeing the ice skaters in the Winter Holiday Special."

"Oh, I'm so glad you saw that," Dr. Snead says. "I think that was one of *my* favorite parts of the Winter Holiday. Just magical."

His cheerfulness is making me mad for some reason. "Well, not really *magical*," I say.

"I'm speaking in hyperbole," says Dr. Snead with a laugh.

Which makes me even more mad, because I don't know what that means. "They were pretty, but it wasn't very deep."

Dr. Snead stops laughing. "What do you mean by that, Hillary?"

"It was just happy, but not . . . more than that." I struggle to find words for what I'm trying to say. "It didn't mean anything."

"You know that happiness isn't a bad thing," Dr. Snead says. "Being happy doesn't make you shallow. It's okay to celebrate happiness, Hillary."

"But there's sad happiness too," I say.

"How do you mean?"

I'm not saying this right. "You know the feeling you get when you're outside alone at night and it's cold and you can see the stars?"

"I usually want to go inside and have some hot chocolate," Dr. Snead says with a smile.

I'm so frustrated. "No, like when you feel really small and everything is bigger than you, and really beautiful, but also kind of scary."

"I'm not sure I'm following you, Hillary."

I shake my head. I'm not smart enough to say this the right way.

"But you should know," he goes on, "that you don't have

to be scared. Or sad. You can be happy."

"It's not all about being happy!" I say loudly.

He looks surprised. I've never raised my voice before.

"That's the problem with everybody, they just want everything to be happy all the time, and we all have to pretend we're happy and nothing's wrong, and we can't talk about anything real, or we'll offend someone or get in trouble. That's why everything is fake, because they pretend all the sad and scary things aren't there—"

Oh man. I've said too much.

Dr. Snead puts his notepad on his desk and folds his hands. "What kind of sad and scary things, Hillary?"

I swallow hard. "Like God."

"Does the idea of God scare you?" he asks.

"Sometimes," I say. I really wish I had just kept my mouth shut.

"What's scary about it?"

"I don't know," I say.

"No, this is good. This is good. You need to express these feelings. Why does God scare you, Hillary?"

"Because maybe He's not good after all," I whisper.

Dr. Snead nods. "That's a valid concern. You've seen some very tragic things happen to people who went to church, prayed, lived Christian lives. If God were good, wouldn't he take care of them?"

I don't know what to say.

"You know what I think, Hillary?" Dr. Snead says.

"What?"

"I think God is the personification of the goodness in human hearts. Maybe we call him God, maybe Allah, maybe Science, maybe Buddha. It doesn't matter what name we call him, because he's universal. God is the love and acceptance inside us. Not something supernatural and scary. When we follow our hearts, we're following God."

"But then why can't we talk about God? Why did I have to change my name?" I ask, confused.

"We do talk about God," Dr. Snead says. "We talk about love, and kindness, and tolerance. We don't use the same language because Christians turned 'God' into something to be scared of, something that condemned people. The Christian God is a God of hell, not heaven."

"But then what about Jesus? Why would He die for people?"

"Jesus was a good man," says Dr. Snead. "He preached against hypocrisy and judging others. There have been many good men, though, who have died for their beliefs. Gandhi. Martin Luther King, Junior."

"But Jesus came back to life," I say.

"In a metaphorical sense. His teachings live on in our hearts."

I'm quiet for a few minutes, considering what he's saying. It seems so easy, so simple, to believe that goodness is just following your heart and being nice to people.

It's flat, though. It's like Winter Holiday instead of Christmas, warm and fuzzy but not real. It's nothing like the rich smell of incense, or the warmth in your throat when you swallow communion, or the brightness of Pascha. I've pulled a bullet from an icon and watched it bleed. Maybe if I had grown up with my grandparents, I could agree with Dr. Snead, but you can't go through what I've been through and not believe in God. The real question is if I want to follow God or not.

"I can tell you don't agree with me," Dr. Snead says.

"I'll think about it," I say.

"That's all I ask," says Dr. Snead with a smile.

In the car on the way home I pull out my phone and find Austin in my contacts. I press the message button by his name.

I want to do this.

—E

FOUR

January 2, 0001 ET

"When I call your name, please come up to my desk and get your new textbook," says Mr. Hill, our Social Studies teacher. "Stanley Allison."

It's the first day back at school, and I still haven't heard anything from Father Innocent. Did he decide it was a bad idea to help me? Did he get caught? I'm supposed to have my phone turned off at school. Instead I have it turned on vibrate so I'll feel it in my pocket if he answers.

"Hillary Booth."

I look up quickly like I always do when someone calls the other Hillary's name. Not my turn yet. Why are we getting new textbooks? We were only a third of the way through the old ones. They were pretty beat up, though. These look new.

"Jeremy DeMarko."

"Austin Hallegher."

"Mr. Hill?" Boston raises her hand.

Mr. Hill pauses in the middle of writing down Austin's name and book number. "Yes?" he says.

"I think you skipped me," Boston says.

Mr. Hill looks at his computer. "I don't have you on here," he says. "That's strange. Let me check . . . oh. They want you to go down to the principal's office."

"Am I in trouble?" Boston says. Her eyes are wide.

"No, no," says Mr. Hill. "I wouldn't worry about it."

Boston stands up and puts her jacket and her backpack on to go. It's so heavy she hunches as she walks to the door.

"And you might want to grab your stuff from your locker before you go," Mr. Hill adds, typing something on his computer.

What, is she never coming back? Some of the other kids must be thinking the same thing, because there are whispers around me, and chairs creak as people shift to look at Boston.

Boston looks like she might cry. She bites her lower lip as she pushes open the heavy door.

"Sheeran Jenson."

"Megan Lang."

Boston pauses and turns to look at Mr. Hill, who is typing, then around the classroom. I feel like somebody ought to say something. Tell her goodbye, or that it's going to be okay. But I'm scared if I say anything, Dr. Snead will hear about it.

"Hillary Matthews," Mr. Hill says.

I get up and go to the front to get my new textbook. Boston and I meet eyes as I pass her, and I wonder if she's still mad at me for throwing rocks.

"Tardell Mitchum."

Mr. Hill hands me my book, and I hear the door shut behind Boston. I sit back down and sit on my hands. I'm cold and shaking a little bit.

The new textbook has a glossy front cover that shows

fingerprints. *An All-New Us: Alabama in the Era of Tolerance.* There's a big picture in the center that shows a black lady and a white lady standing with a bunch of smiling kids under an Alabama state flag. And then a lot of little darker pictures on the sides of people fighting in the streets, men in white hoods, burning crosses, and graffiti on a sign that says "Emergency Pregnancy Clinic."

I open the textbook to the first page. There's a preface.

A New Alabama

Alabama is a state rich in culture and tradition. We value our history and our heritage. So how do we move forward into the Era of Tolerance without losing sight of where we've been? The answer, of course, lies in studying our past and identifying the sources of prejudice and contempt that led to so much turmoil. We will address religion in particular and its rejection of equality for—

I jump in my seat as I feel my pocket buzz. I raise my hand. "Mr. Hill?" I ask.

"Yes, Hillary?"

"May I use the restroom?"

"Hurry back."

Mr. Hill hands me the hall pass, and I hurry out. I run straight into some people walking in the other direction, towards the school exit.

"Oh, sorry," I mumble, backing up against the lockers.

"It's fine," the man says automatically, brushing off his suit.

It's the man from the library. The one with the pink skin

and white hair, the one that was telling Mimi to get rid of all the Christian books. There's another man with him, shorter and more muscular, who's holding onto Boston. Not by her hand, but by her wrist. They walk off down the hallway, and Boston shoots me a terrified look.

I stand frozen against the lockers, clutching the hall pass, until they're gone. Then I run to the girls' room, shut myself in a stall, and pull out my phone. There's a new message from Father Innocent.

I think you and Carter Wesson would be good friends.

I scroll down. That's it? Carter Wesson and I would be good friends? Really? Who the heck is Carter Wesson? There's nothing else, nothing about the icon or Orthodoxy or anything. I jam my phone back into my pocket and kick the stall door open. This is stupid. I thought he was going to help me.

January 3, 0001 ET

Mimi isn't in the juvenile section. Or the nonfiction. Or behind the front desk or in the media room or anywhere else she usually is. Maybe she doesn't work on Wednesdays? Grandma couldn't bring me yesterday because of her hair appointment. When I go to the back of the library to peek in the "Employees Only" room, I hear someone say her name. I edge closer to the door to listen.

"Anyway, I'm sorry you had to come in at the last minute, but when she didn't show up, I really needed someone to help out."

"No worries. Do you think she'll be here tomorrow?"

"I doubt it. In fact, if you're interested in changing to full-time, you should send an application to city hall."

What? Is Mimi gone?

"Did she resign?" the other voice seems just as surprised as I am.

"Not officially, but I highly doubt she'll come back after yesterday. I caught her altering patron records for those lists the rep from DRT wanted. It's a good thing I did see them before she sent them out; she had just copied and pasted one barcode over and over, and it turned out to be the guy's own card."

Someone laughs. "Yeah, that wouldn't have gone over well."

"No. And anyway, I can't find any of those books the Department of Religious Tolerance wanted her to pull. She was supposed to put them in the dumpster out back, but the only thing there was the *Elsie Dinsmoor* collection. I'll have to report her for stealing."

"That's crazy. Man, you think you know someone."

"I know . . . oh, crud, it's already five till . . . I need to get back up front."

The doorknob turns, and I duck quickly into the bathroom next door. I stand against the wall beside the trash can for a minute, breathing hard and listening. When everything's quiet outside, I slide down the wall and let myself stare at the sink for a while, pulling my fingers. Mimi's gone, and she never said goodbye.

January 4, 0001 ET

I don't have to go see Dr. Snead today because I'm throwing up. I wake up sick, with a really bad headache, and soon I'm sitting in front of the toilet with my hair pulled back in a ponytail, shivering and wishing it were over.

Grandma comes after a while. I guess the sound woke her up. I'm rinsing my mouth in the sink when she walks in.

"Are you sick, honey?" she asks, rubbing my back.

I nod, spitting out the water and turning off the faucet. I'm shaking really bad.

"Why didn't you wake me up?" she asks.

I shrug and sit back down in front of the toilet.

Grandma doesn't say anything for a minute and then pats my shoulder. "I'll be right back."

I stare at the hole in the bottom of the toilet and try not to think about anything until she returns. *Lord Jesus Christ, have mercy on me, Lord Jesus Christ, have mercy on me, Lord Jesus Christ, have mercy on me.* Is it wrong to say the Jesus Prayer because you don't want to throw up?

When Grandma comes in again, she has the fuzzy brown blanket from the couch, a bottle of Pepto-Bismol, and a can of her Diet Coke. She wraps the blanket around my shoulders and measures out a little of the pink medicine. "See if you can drink this," she says.

I swallow the medicine, but a minute later I feel sick again. Grandma rubs my back as I lean over the toilet and then helps me stand so I can wash out my mouth.

"Maybe we'll wait a while before you try and keep anything down," Grandma says. "Goodness, you're shaking. Here, lean against the tub and try to take deep breaths."

I nod and sit back. Grandma doesn't have any of her makeup on, and her short, grey hair is sticking up in the back. She looks nicer to me than she ever does in the daylight. She has smile wrinkles around her eyes and the corners of her mouth, and for the first time I notice how much her nose is like Dad's. And like mine.

"What's that book you're reading right now?" she asks. "The one about time?"

"*A Wrinkle in Time*," I manage to say.

"Do you want me to get it for you?" she asks. "I could read some of it out loud."

I nod again.

When she comes back from my bedroom she has a weird expression on her face, but I'm feeling so sick I don't want to ask her what's wrong. She lowers herself slowly onto the fuzzy bathmat by the sink and then opens the book. "Where did you leave off?"

I'm too sick to answer.

She starts at the beginning. "It was a dark and stormy night."

January 5, 0001 ET

"Hey," the boy says.

I turn around from where I was leaning against the soccer field fence and staring at the woods.

I've seen him before, but I don't know his name. He's a seventh-grader, but he's not in any of my classes. He's got medium brown hair, pale skin, and freckles.

"Hey," I say back.

He holds out his hand. "I'm Carter," he says. "Are you Hillary?"

"Yeah," I say, shaking his hand awkwardly. What kind of twelve-year-old shakes hands when they meet a kid at break?

He grins. "Someone said we should be friends."

It clicks in my head. "Wait, are you Carter Wesson?"

"Yeah," he says. He lowers his voice. "But really I'm Alex."

"That was my Dad's name!" I say. "And also Mimi's husband."

"Who's Mimi?"

"She was my friend," I say. "But I'm not sure where she is now. Her real name was Mary."

"Mary Russell?"

"I don't know. She used to work at the library."

"Yeah, that's Mary Russell!" Alex says. "I know her! She usually comes on Sundays. She's in the choir."

"Wait, what's on Sundays?" I ask.

Alex suddenly looks serious. He glances around, but

there's no one near us on the field. "Hey, you're . . . I mean, you aren't gonna say anything, are you?" he asks. "Cause Father told me I could trust you."

"You can trust me," I say.

Alex leans forward. "Secret liturgy," he whispers.

"What?" I whisper back. "There's still liturgy? People are still going?"

He nods. "You should come. If your grandparents will let you. You can tell them you're invited to my house to hang out and watch movies or something." He hands me a scrap of paper. It has a phone number written on it. His handwriting is really bad—it looks like a four-year-old wrote it.

"I have texting now," he says. "I got a new phone for Christmas."

"Cool, me too," I say. I put the paper in my pocket. "I'll ask my Grandma if I can come over. What time?"

"Like nine-fifteen on Sunday," Alex says. "It really starts at ten, but we leave our house at nine-thirty."

"Okay."

"I'll see you then," Alex says and shakes my hand again. He walks off with his hands in his pockets and goes back to a bunch of boys who are choosing teams for kickball. A couple of them laugh, and one punches him playfully in the arm.

When I get home, I put Alex's number in my phone and open up a blank message. Then I can't think of anything to say. I don't want to write anything about liturgy in case someone reads it, but we didn't really talk about anything else. Maybe I shouldn't text him. I don't know. Should I?

I	C
O	N

In the end I send him a smiley face and then wish I hadn't.

January 7, 0001 ET

On Sunday morning I come down to get something to eat and find Grandma scooping balls of cookie dough onto a pan.

"Whoa, cookies?" I say. I stand next to her to watch and then smell the batch that is already getting gooey and warm in the oven. "For breakfast?"

Grandma gives me a big hug. "No, silly! I thought you could take them with you to the Wessons' house. Are you excited about going over to work on your project with Carter?"

Actually I'm really nervous. And I feel bad about lying to Grandma. And his name isn't even Carter. But she looks so happy that I'm going to another kid's house. I never hang out with anybody from school. "Yeah, I guess," I say. I try to steal some cookie dough from the mixing bowl, and Grandma swats my hand away.

"Go find something healthy to eat," she says.

"Cookies are more exciting."

"We have Lucky Charms. And Pop-tarts."

"How is that better than cookies?" I say.

"You can't eat cookies for breakfast," says Grandma, shaking her head.

"Can you make me homemade soup?" I ask. Hot soup sounds pretty good.

"Good grief, Hillie-billie, just make yourself some toast or something!" Grandma laughs.

I trudge over to the pantry and get out the box of Pop-tarts. There's only one pack left. I take the pastries out of the silver wrapper and put them in a napkin. "I'm gonna go figure out what I'm gonna wear," I say.

Grandma is busy getting the first tray of cookies out of the oven and doesn't hear me. It looks like she's making a lot.

I try on three outfits in my room before I decide on the blue dress and gray sweater that I got for Christmas. It feels weird to be getting ready for church. I almost wear my black maryjanes that are a little too small for me, but then I remember I'll probably be standing up for a long time. Better wear my boots.

"You look nice," Grandma says when I come back downstairs.

Grandpa cranes his head to see me from his recliner in the living room. "Very pretty," he says. "Ask your Grandma for some of her makeup stuff. You won't even be able to see that pimple on your chin." He sits back and opens his newspaper.

"Richard," Grandma protests.

I feel my chin, and sure enough there's a tiny bump that hurts when I touch it. I run to the bathroom.

It's small but bright red. The more I look at it, the more it stands out. I squeeze it a little, and the skin around it turns pink.

"Hillary?" Grandma sticks her head in.

"I've got a pimple," I say. I poke it again and wince. It hurts. How did I not feel it before?

"It's so small, no one will notice," Grandma says.

"Grandpa noticed," I say. I can feel tears coming. This is not something to cry about. This is not something to cry about.

"I really don't think anyone will care," Grandma says. "But if it makes you self-conscious, you can go get a little of my concealer and cover it. It's that cream-colored stuff in the tube on my sink."

I go up to Grandma's bathroom and try to make the pimple less noticeable. The concealer covers up the redness, but I can still see the bump. And it still hurts when I touch it. I don't feel pretty anymore. I go back into my room and zip up my puffy brown coat over my dress and sweater.

"She's sensitive," Grandma's voice comes from the living room as I walk back downstairs.

"Well, she needs to toughen up," Grandpa says.

"It's a hard age, Richard—"

Grandma stops talking as she hears me. "You ready to go, Hillie-billie?" she asks.

"Yeah, I guess," I say, looking at the floor.

"Do you think you need that big jacket? It's not very cold today."

I shrug.

"Well, it's up to you," Grandma says. She grabs the tin of cookies from the kitchen and we head out to the car.

Alex's house is in a nice neighborhood. It takes us half an hour to get there. At first we can't find it because the street numbers on the mailboxes are so fancy they're hard to read, but finally the door to a big white house with green shutters opens, and a boy with brown hair and freckles comes out and waves to us from the porch.

"Is that Carter?" Grandma asks, pulling the car into the driveway.

"Yeah," I say. "Whoa, their house is really big."

"It's nice," Grandma says. "I want to ask about that climbing rose on the trellis. I've been looking for something that blooms during the wintertime." She unbuckles her seatbelt and unlocks her door.

"Oh, you don't have to come in," I say quickly. What if they think Grandma is Orthodox? Or have icons up or something?

"I want to talk to Mrs. Wesson," Grandma says, opening her door and stepping out. "She was so nice when we spoke on the phone. And I want to meet Carter."

I get out quickly and hurry up the sidewalk behind her.

"Hi, Mrs. Matthews," Alex says when she gets to the porch. He gives her a big smile and shakes her hand. "I'm Carter."

"Very nice to meet you, Carter," Grandma says. "We brought you all some cookies—oh! Hillary, can you run and grab that tin of cookies from the car?"

"Sure," I say.

"So how did you and Hillary get to be friends?" Grandma

asks as I run back to get the cookies. I can't hear what Alex says, but it must be good, because Grandma is laughing when I get back.

The door opens as I walk up the steps, and Mrs. Wesson comes out. She's very short, barely taller than me, and she's pregnant. It's kind of weird-looking because she's so small—like she's got a watermelon under her dress. She's still really pretty, though. She's got freckles like Alex.

"You must be Hillary and Mrs. Matthews!" she says.

"Oh, call me Gladys," Grandma says. "It's so nice to meet you!"

They start talking about me and Alex and how great it is we're friends now and all kinds of embarrassing stuff, and Alex makes a funny stressed-out face at me. I make my eyes really wide and give a crazy-person smile in answer.

"Wanna see my room?" Alex asks.

"Sure," I say.

He ducks under his mom's arm, and I follow him inside.

It's a nice house. All shiny wood floors and white curtains and indoor plants, and the smell of rich people. I can never figure out what that smell is. Maybe they all use the same kind of detergent. I wish I could stop and look at everything, but Alex takes me straight upstairs to a door that has a big yellow sign on it, like the ones you see on the side of the road where there are crosswalks.

"What's that?" I say, pointing to the lumpy black silhouette on the sign.

"Oh, that's a narwhal."

"A what?"

"A narwhal," Alex says. "It's like a cross between a whale and a unicorn. Pretty awesome." He opens the door for me and stands aside.

"Whoa," I say.

Alex's room is not like the rest of the house. For one thing, it's super messy. There are clothes and books and Legos and half-empty soda bottles all over the floor. The walls are covered with posters and realtor signs with beards and mustaches drawn on the people's faces. He's got a bunk bed with a bunch of pillows shaped like pizza slices. The bottom bunk is hidden by a blanket-curtain.

"You wanna draw on my ceiling?" he asks.

I laugh. "What?"

Then I see that the ceiling above the top bunk is covered in doodles.

"That's awesome!" I say. We climb up the ladder and onto the bed. He's got a huge pack of markers up there and everything. "I can't believe you're allowed to do this," I say, uncapping a green marker and starting to write.

"I know, right?" Alex says, picking up a brown marker. "My dad wants to repaint the ceiling, so he said I could draw on it if I wanted to. What are you writing?"

"Afro seen," I say.

It's his turn to laugh. "What?"

"Afro seen," I repeat.

He cranes his head to see. "What's that supposed to mean?"

"It's my real name," I say. "Euphrosyne. In case somebody else looks up here." I draw a little guy with a 'fro and a pair of glasses underneath the words.

"Sweet," Alex says. He lies on his back and starts drawing a giant chicken.

After a few minutes Mrs. Wesson comes and opens the door. "Almost time to go, guys. Alex! This room is such a mess! I told you to clean it up for Hillary!"

"I did. It just got messy again," Alex says. "By the way, her real name's Euphrosyne."

Mrs. Wesson sighs. "Nice to meet you, Euphrosyne," she says. "I'm sorry Alex's room looks like a hurricane came through."

"I don't mind," I say.

Alex gives me a thumbs-up. "Her room is probably messy too, right, Euphrosyne?"

"Actually it's pretty clean right now," I answer apologetically.

"Well, I have dyslexia," Alex says.

I laugh, and Alex's mom says, "That has nothing to do with it. Now come on, we're gonna be late."

We clamber back down the ladder.

"Are you going in jeans?" I ask Alex. He's got holes in the knees of his pants, and his shirt has a Minecraft guy on it.

"Yeah, in case we get pulled over," he says. "The police stop more people on Sundays, so we always take water and say we're going hiking."

"Oh." I wish I hadn't worn a dress.

Mr. Wesson waits by the front door with a six-pack of water bottles under his arm. He's really tall and has blond hair and a short, reddish beard. He gives Mrs. Wesson a peck on the lips and then checks his watch. "We need to go," he says. "Are we waiting on Jenny?"

"No, I think she's sleeping in at her friend's house," Mrs. Wesson says.

"Is Jenny your sister?" I ask Alex.

He makes a face. "Yeah. She doesn't come to liturgy much anymore."

"Oh." I don't know what to say to that.

The Wessons have a green van with two rows of back seats. Alex and I sit right behind his mom and dad, with the middle seat empty so we don't accidentally bump hands or something. Mrs. Wesson asks me a lot of questions during the drive, about school and what I like to do. She seems really nice.

The drive is about half an hour, but it seems longer. We leave the city and go deeper and deeper into the country, finally turning onto a dirt road that winds around for miles. The van bounces and rattles over potholes and rocks. I feel a little sick by the time we pull into a little clearing with a trailer and five or six other cars. Mr. Wesson parks in back, and we all climb out of the van.

As the van doors slam I hear another sound, one that sends shivers up my spine. A sound that I haven't heard in months. Bells are ringing inside the trailer. Orthodox bells. Sad and joyful and angry and amazed, all at the same time.

Like the bells themselves know everything that's happened and are singing about it.

"I'm gonna hurry—I've got to find my robe and get a blessing," Alex says to his dad. He half runs across the yard and around to the front of the trailer. The rest of us follow more slowly. I've got my arms wrapped around myself tightly and I'm suddenly cold, even though it's not that bad outside. I can't believe that this is happening. That this place exists.

Mr. Wesson leads the way up the wooden steps and opens the door. Mrs. Wesson and I follow him in.

It all hits me in a wave. The thick, foreign smell of incense. The heat of bodies and candles. The jingle of the censer. The people inside turn to see who's come in, and for a second I can't tell between the faces of the congregation and the faces of the icons hanging on the walls. They all swim together. My right hand travels up to my forehead almost on its own and draws the sign of the cross over my body.

Mrs. Wesson pulls the door closed behind us and steps in front of me beside Mr. Wesson to cross herself and bow three times. They walk forward down the center of the long room and start to venerate the icon displayed on a stand in the middle. I hurry to make my three bows. I'm out of practice. I venerate the icon in the middle shakily and then walk to the front of the room to kiss the icons of Christ and the Theotokos. Through a panel of larger icons on easels ahead of me, I can see the priest and three altar boys robed in gold, moving around the altar.

I go to stand with Mr. and Mrs. Wesson on the right side

of the trailer. It's been months since I was in church, but my body knows what to do—feet together, hands clasped in front of me, knees bent a little so I won't pass out, eyes wide to take everything in.

The priest appears in the center gap of the row of icons. I get a glimpse of the silver and black beard before he turns to the altar. It's Father Innocent.

"Blessed is the kingdom," he sings, "of the Father, and of the Son, and of the Holy Spirit . . . now and ever, and unto ages of ages."

"Amen," voices from the corner of the trailer sing.

"In peace let us pray to the Lord," sings Father Innocent.

"Lord have mercy."

I sneak a glance over to the corner. There are four or five people in the choir. I give a little gasp as I recognize two of them. Mimi stands at the edge of the group, staring down at a binder of sheet music, her face partly shadowed by her black headscarf. Standing next to her is a dark-skinned young man with a short beard and a voice that I recognize right away. It's Daniel Liakos, Mr. Liakos's oldest son. I thought he was safe in Europe somewhere.

I have to wait till after liturgy to talk to Mimi. I shift impatiently. I want to go up and give her a big hug. Maybe she'll look my way and I can wave.

We sing through the first section of songs—I can't remember what they're called. I should know. Dad used to tell me and Kat about parts of the service and what they mean, but I guess I wasn't listening very well. It's the songs with the parts about "blessed are the persecuted" and "blessed are the pure in heart" and also the one with "Who art risen from the dead!" which I always sing really loud because I know those parts. And the "Holy God" song that always sounds so sad, where we all bow three times.

Everything seems extra mysterious and strange after being away from church for so long. For the first time I realize I don't understand much of what's going on. I've always loved it, but I never wondered before about where all the parts of the liturgy came from. What's a *prokeimenon,* anyway? Why do we repeat everything a bunch of times?

My legs are getting tired. I'm not used to standing up for a long time anymore. I'm glad when it's time for Father Innocent to talk for a little bit and we can sit and listen. He talks about Jesus being baptized and the Holy Spirit coming down. "Christ is Baptized!" he says.

"In the River Jordan!" everybody answers, and I answer too, even though I'd forgotten that I knew the response to that.

We stand up again, and the choir sings about the cherubim while Father Innocent and the altar boys walk around the outside of the room and pray for everyone. There's a lot more in the liturgy—the Lord's Prayer and saying the Creed and everyone lining up to take Communion. I don't get in line because I'm not sure if I'm supposed to or not. I haven't been fasting or confessing or praying or going to church—what if I went up there and Father Innocent had to tell me in front of everybody not to commune? I'd rather wait and ask him later what I should do.

Before the service ends, we sing "Many Years" for all the people who have birthdays, and then "Memory Eternal" for all the people who have died. Father Innocent reads out a lot of names for that one. I hear five Alexes and two Nicoles and a Child Katerina in the list, and I wonder if those are my family members, if they've been prayed for all this time.

When liturgy is over, we all get in line to kiss the gold cross and get a blessing from Father Innocent. I'm a little nervous, but he just holds out the cross for me to kiss and says, "God bless you," in that same quiet voice he used when he told me Merry Christmas in the bookshop. By the time I get through the line, Mimi has disappeared, and the Wessons are ready to go home. Father hasn't said anything to me about getting back the St. Nicholas icon or what I should do now that Alex and I are friends.

I go home feeling more confused than ever.

January 9, 0001 ET

Grandpa orders pizza for dinner. It's a big deal, because Grandma almost always makes dinner for us. But tonight she's going out with a couple of other ladies to a restaurant or something. So it's just me and Grandpa.

"How was school today?" Grandpa says, opening his beer.

"It was okay," I say through a mouthful of pizza. "I did good on my vocab quiz from Friday."

"That's my girl," Grandpa nods. "How's that math stuff coming?"

I swallow my bite of pizza and take another. It's really good. I'm not concentrating on what I'm saying. "It's fine right now," I say. "We're just reviewing stuff from before Christmas break. I think next week we're starting a new chapter in the book, though. It looks hard."

Grandpa sits back in his chair and squints his eyes at me. It takes me a minute to realize something's wrong. He looks mad. I put down my piece of pizza. What'd I do? We were just talking, and everything was fine.

"Grandpa?" I say timidly. "It's just math. I'll figure it out."

"You still saying stuff like that?" he asks over me.

"What?" I'm confused.

"Your Grandma worries about you a lot, you know," Grandpa says. "We took you in and took care of you when your dad screwed up and got himself killed, and we feed you and take you to school and some fancy shrink, and you go on talking about Christmas and arguing with him about God and Jesus and who knows what else. What's wrong with you?"

I don't know what to say. My heart's beating really fast.

Grandpa slams his beer down on the table. "I said, *what's wrong with you?*" he growls.

"I'm sorry . . ." I whisper.

"Sorry doesn't fix it," Grandpa says. "You wanna get us all killed? Like your mom and dad? You think all that's over now?"

"No," I say. My voice is squeaky.

"Good, cause it's not," Grandpa says. "You keep talking the way you do, we're gonna get arrested or shot or who knows what. You gotta quit that, Euphrosyne."

"What?" I ask, shaken.

"I said you gotta quit that," Grandpa says.

"But you called me Euphrosyne," I say.

"No I didn't," Grandpa says. "Don't say that name."

"But you called me that!"

"I did not call you that," Grandpa says. He stands up, and his chair falls over behind him. "Don't disrespect me, Hillary."

I'm getting mad. "I'm not Hillary," I say. "And you know it too—you called me Euphrosyne."

"I said, don't disrespect me!" Grandpa shouts. He grabs me by my arm and pulls me out of my chair.

"Ow!" I cry. He walks me upstairs, dragging me a little bit when I trip on one of the steps. "You're hurting me!"

"I'm teaching you what's gonna save your life," Grandpa says. He kicks open the door to my room and slings me onto my bed.

I shrink away from him, clutching my arm. The skin is all red where his hand was.

Grandpa opens my backpack and dumps my books and stuff onto the floor. He searches the pockets and dumps out my pens and pencils and gum wrappers. He starts jerking drawers out of my desk and throwing all the stuff onto the pile.

"No!" I cry as he grabs the handle of the top left drawer.

IC
O N

Grandpa yanks the drawer open and pulls out *A Wrinkle in Time*. He tosses it aside and reaches into the back. And says a bad word.

His hand comes out holding two of the little figures from the Nativity set. Baby Jesus and the Theotokos. He drops them on the desk and pulls out the angel with the broken wing. "I should have known you'd do that," he says.

I stare at the little people lying helplessly on my desk and feel everything falling apart around me.

"Hold out your hand," Grandpa says.

I don't move. I'm scared to.

"I said, hold out your hand," Grandpa repeats in a scary voice.

I hold my hand out shakily.

Grandpa puts the Baby Jesus in my palm. It's cold against my skin. Baby Jesus' eyes are closed peacefully like He's asleep.

"Break it," Grandpa says.

"What?"

"I said break it," he repeats.

I look at the little baby's face and back at Grandpa's.

"It's a piece of china!" Grandpa yells. "You care more about some stupid thing than me or your Grandma? Break it, Hillary!" He grabs the Theotokos off my desk and throws her against the wall. She shatters into bits of painted porcelain.

I start crying. But I don't want to break the Baby Jesus.

Grandpa reaches for the figurine. I try to keep it from him, but he pries it out of my fingers and hurls it away. I hear it smash.

"Stop crying," Grandpa says.

I cry even harder.

"I said, stop it," Grandpa says. "Grow up. You gotta learn to survive in this world."

I sob and sob, staring at him like he's turned into a monster or something. How could this be happening?

"You gotta learn," Grandpa says. He grabs me by the shoulders and shakes me back and forth. "You gotta learn, Hillary!"

"I'm not Hillary!" I scream at him.

Grandpa slaps me on the face.

It stings so bad that for a second I stop crying and just clutch my hand to my burning skin.

$$\begin{array}{c|c} \text{I} & \text{C} \\ \hline \text{O} & \text{N} \end{array}$$

Grandpa straightens up, breathing hard. I can't even look at his face. "You gotta learn," he says quietly. He takes the angel off my desk and walks out of my room, rubbing the back of his neck.

FIVE

January 10, 0001 ET

Grandma comes into my room at 6:45 because I haven't gotten up yet.

"Hillary, wake up," she says. "Whoa, this room is a mess. Did you sleep with the light on last night?"

"Yeah," I say from under the covers. I just want to stay here. I just want everyone to leave me alone.

I hear Grandma moving around and opening my curtains. She stops near the wall where the broken pieces of porcelain are. I keep waiting for her to say something, but she doesn't. She just comes and sits on my bed. Maybe she's waiting for me to talk first. I don't want to talk or think. Just hide under the covers.

Finally she gives me a little pat on the arm. I wince. I think it's bruised.

"I'm gonna get some coffee going," she says. "You want to stop by McDonald's and pick up breakfast on the way to school?"

"Yeah," I say.

She gets up to go.

"Hey, Grandma?"

"Uh-huh?"

"Did Grandpa leave for work already?"

"Yeah, he left early today," Grandma says.

I hear her stand there for another minute, waiting for me to say something else. Then she goes downstairs.

When I go to the bathroom, I find a purple bruise on my arm and a red mark on my left cheek. I use some of Grandma's concealer to make my face look normal and put on a long-sleeved shirt to hide my arm. It takes a while to squeeze all my books and binders and stuff into my backpack again.

We go by McDonald's on the way to school, and I get an egg and cheese McMuffin, which seems like a good idea until I bite into it and realize that the last one I had was on Pascha with Mr. Liakos. I try to finish it so Grandma doesn't feel bad, but my stomach feels queasy. In the end I'm glad to get out of the car and head into the school, where nobody will pay any attention to me.

It's a boring Wednesday. Miss Linda hands out the classroom journals that she wants us to write in for the rest of the semester and tells us we can write about whatever we want, and she'll keep it private. I already know that's a lie, because she tells Dr. Snead everything, so I write about how I like my new clothes I got for Winter Holiday and how I want to be a fashion designer when I grow up.

I don't actually know what I want to be when I grow up, but the other girls in my class are always talking about how they want to be fashion designers and how their moms say they're so talented, so it seems like a safe lie. I draw some pictures of dresses and shoes at the bottom of the page to make it look convincing.

On the picnic grounds, I sit on the wooden ledge that keeps all the pebbles in and tuck my hands inside my jacket pockets to keep them warm. I stare through the links of the fence at the forest and let my mind wander.

"Yo, Euphrosyne!"

I jump.

Alex plops down next to me. "How's it going?" he says.

I look around to see if there's anyone nearby. "Don't call me that here!" I hiss. "We could get in huge trouble!"

"I made sure no one's around," Alex says, shrugging.

"Just don't call me that here."

"Dang, you're grumpy today."

"Look, this whole thing is really serious," I tell him. "You've got to be careful. We probably shouldn't even be talking."

"I know it's serious," he says. "But come on, we're kids. Nobody's paying attention to us."

"Yeah, they are," I say. "They're all watching me. You should go hang out with somebody else, or they'll start watching you, too."

"We're supposed to be friends, remember?" Alex points out. "It's normal for us to hang out. Otherwise it'd be weird that you come over to my house."

I shift a little so we aren't sitting so close. "Well, try and act normal then. Don't call me that name here."

Alex laughs. "You're the one who isn't acting normal! Just relax." He gives me a little punch in the arm.

"Ow!" I say.

"Oh, come on, that didn't hurt," he says.

I clutch the place where Grandpa held onto me and feel tears well up in my eyes. "Just leave me alone," I tell him. I'm about to start crying. Please let him go away. "I'm not feeling good."

"Hey, I'm sorry," Alex says. "Did that really hurt? I'm sorry, I didn't mean to . . ."

He really does look sorry. I start feeling bad for making *him* feel bad when it wasn't his fault, and then all confused because I'm feeling too many things at once, and a tear runs down my cheek. "It's fine," I mumble. "I just want to be alone."

"Okay," Alex says. "I'm really sorry." He stands up and waits awkwardly for a minute, like he's not sure if he should give me a hug or apologize again or what.

I just bite my lip and try to focus on not crying.

After a minute Alex shoves his hands in his pockets and walks away with his head down. I pull up the hood of my jacket and stare at the forest.

January 11, 0001 ET

"Welcome back, Hillary," Dr. Snead says. His hair is back to normal, gelled flat against his skull. He sits down in his chair and opens my file. "It's been a while since I've seen you. Are you feeling better?"

"Yeah," I say.

"Looks like you've had a good couple of weeks at school," he says. "Anything special happen since we've talked?"

Um. Mimi disappeared. Boston disappeared. I met Alex and his family. I went to my first liturgy in months. Mimi reappeared. My Grandpa found my secret stuff and smashed everything and hit me.

"I don't know," I say.

Dr. Snead gives a chuckle, but he looks kind of annoyed. "Now, let's not start off with the 'I don't know' thing. If you don't want to talk about it, just say so."

"I don't want to talk about it."

"Why not?"

"I just don't."

"Come on, Hillary, you can be honest with me. We had such a good discussion last time. I feel like you really opened up and shared your thoughts. And didn't talking about your worries help you deal with them?"

"No," I say.

He looks at me long and hard, furrowing his eyebrows. Then he closes my file and sets it on his desk. He leans forward on his elbows so his face is closer to mine. "Something happened, didn't it?" he asks quietly.

I don't say anything, just stare back at him.

"Something *did* happen," he says. "You know how I can tell, Hillary? Because you're mad."

I still don't say anything.

"When you first started coming to see me, you were anxious all the time. You were scared. You were twitchy and you pulled on your fingers, and you were always very shy." He's staring at me without blinking. I feel my left eye itch, but I feel like if I shut it, I'll lose.

"You know what, Hillary?" Dr. Snead says. "You haven't pulled your fingers at all today. And you're not shaking. You aren't afraid, you're angry."

I want to clap my hands in his face and make him blink.

"Did you get in a fight with your new friend? What's his name . . . Carter?"

"Mind your own—" (I say my first ever bad word) "—business."

Dr. Snead laughs and slaps his knee like I said something really funny.

I squeeze my hands into fists. I had meant it to sound intimidating. Now I just look like a stupid kid. I probably didn't even use the word right.

"You've changed so much, Hillary," Dr. Snead says, still laughing. "I'm impressed with how much you're growing! You've got so much more confidence than you used to."

"I just said a bad word," I say, "and you're happy about it."

"It's a sign that you're getting more mature," Dr. Snead

said. "And expressing your feelings."

"No it's not. It's just a stupid, bad word, and I shouldn't have said it."

"It's okay to cuss, Hillary."

"No, it's not!" I say again. "I'm just a kid!"

"Even kids need to have freedom to express themselves."

Then why are you watching everything I do and say? I ask silently. I'm getting really upset, and if I keep talking, I know I'll give something away.

"It's okay to use language, Hillary," Dr. Snead repeats when he can tell I've shut up for good. "You can always use whatever words make you feel better."

He has a strange, eager look in his eye. Like he wants me to say the word again. Like it would mean he is finally getting to me.

I don't say anything for the rest of the session, and we end early. When I leave with Grandma, I feel dirty and depressed. Because Dr. Snead was right. The old Hillary—I mean, Euphrosyne—would never have said something like that.

January 12, 0001 ET

It's 10:10 pm when my phone buzzes.

I'm half asleep already, and I jerk upright in my bed. I take my phone out from under my pillow. It's glowing, and there's a text from a number I don't recognize. I swipe the screen to pull up the message.

Have you finished A Wrinkle in Time?

I stare at the screen. Other than Grandma and Grandpa, there's only one person who would know about me reading that.

Yes, I send back.

The little dots appear on the screen. She's typing something.

WEE ARRE HEERRREEE

I laugh.

I wish I could tesser, I type.

Where would you go?

Anywhere but here.

She answers with a little frowny face. *That bad?*

Yeah.

The little dots appear, then vanish, then pop up again, then vanish again. She can't decide what to say next.

I saw you singing, I type.

I heard you were there! she says. *I was so mad I missed you! Are you coming back?*

I think so.

Good.

Where are you now? I ask.

There's a little pause. *I don't want to answer that over text*, she says.

Oh. Okay. That makes sense. I type, *I wish I could live with you.*

Another frowny face. *Your grandparents seem like good people.*

My Grandma's nice, I send.

Not so much your Grandpa?

He hit me the other day cause he found out I was hiding stuff, I answer. She's the first person I've told.

The dots appear and vanish a couple of times before I get an answer.

That makes me really mad. I want to come pick you up right now. Are you okay?

I'm okay, I text back. My heart's racing. She wants to come get me?

Are your grandparents asleep?

I don't know. Just a sec. I put down the phone and tiptoe across my room. When I crack open my bedroom door, I hear Grandpa snoring. They go to bed early for grownups. I sneak back to my bed and pick up the phone. *Yeah, they are.*

I can be there in about an hour. Can you get some clothes packed and sneak out of the house without waking them up?

Yeah, I answer. I can feel my heart beating even faster.

What's your address?

I send it to her.

Okay. Do you know how to wipe your phone clean? she asks.

No. I add a frowny face.

She sends me instructions. *You'll have to leave it at your grandparents' house, or they can track it,* she says.

Okay.

I'll see you in a little bit.

Okay.

I turn the flashlight on my phone on and start taking all the books out of my backpack. I cram in all my underwear and socks and two pairs of jeans and two shirts, and I change out of my pajamas and into my last pair of jeans and a sweatshirt and my jacket. There's no room for extra shoes, so I'll only have the tennis shoes I'm wearing. I put my hair up in a ponytail and then erase everything on my phone and leave it on my pillow.

Are we really doing this? I feel jumpy and skittish.

Grandpa's snoring doesn't stop as I creep down the stairs. Everything is quiet. The clock on the microwave glows a sleepy green. I can't believe I'm running away. I unlock the front door and slip out.

It's a cold and silent January night. I sit down by the garbage can at the end of the driveway, wrap my arms around my knees, and wait. The stars are as wide-eyed and mysterious as they were the night it snowed. The cold seeps up from the concrete and through my pants.

I'm starting to get sleepy again by the time a beat-up white car turns onto our street. For a minute I'm not sure if I should run and hide. If it's not her, it might be weird to see a kid sitting out by a garbage can in the middle of the night.

The car slows down and stops in front of the house. I stand up and sling my backpack on again as the light inside the car flickers on. It's Mimi.

January 13, 0001 ET

The room is chilly, even though there's sunlight coming through the window. My blankets are warm, though. And heavy. Especially right over my feet for some reason. I pull my knees in close to my body and hear a *snorgling* sound, almost like a pig would make, from the foot of the bed. When I peek over the patchwork quilt, I see a black-and-white dog with a squished-up nose looking at me in a hurt way.

"Sorry," I whisper.

The dog snorgles again and crawls up to lick my chin.

"Ew. Quit," I say.

He looks so disappointed that I let him slobber on my fingers for a few minutes. He keeps blinking at me sideways and snorgling and squirming. He's almost like a pig, with a little piglet body and a pig nose and triangle-shaped ears. And thin little legs.

"You're weird," I tell him.

The dog opens his mouth and grins at me. Just like the dog in *Because of Winn-Dixie*! "You should be named Walmart or Publix or something," I tell him. "Or Piggly-Wiggly. Ha."

I look around for a clock in the room, but I don't see one. There are lots of books piled against all the walls, except for where the bed is and a bedside table with some candles and a copy of a book called *Till We Have Faces*. When I sit up, I see that Mimi's in a sleeping bag on the floor, with her head on a couch cushion and her hands curled up in front of her face. Her breathing is slow and deep.

Where are we? It was too dark to see anything last night. I lean forward to look through the window, and all I can see is tree branches.

The drive last night seemed to last forever. I think I fell asleep, because I barely remember Mimi shaking me and telling me we were here. And then stumbling through the dark and waiting while she tried to find the right key to open the door.

It's starting to sink in that I actually ran away. No one besides Mimi knows where I am. Is Grandma worried? Will she call the police? What will the school do when I don't show up? What will Dr. Snead do?

I hug the pig dog for comfort, and he snorts and squirms some more, trying to twist around to lick my face.

Mimi stirs on the floor. The dog hears her and wiggles out of my arms to jump off the bed and lick Mimi's face instead.

"Uggh, Wart, quit. You're so gross," she says, pushing the dog's snout out of her face.

I giggle. "Wart?" I ask.

"It's a literary reference," she mumbles, rubbing her eyes.

Wart hears us talking about him and smiles again. He sits down and looks back and forth between us. If he were Hershey, I bet he would be thumping his tail on the ground. I don't think Wart even has a tail. He grunts happily.

"Why does he keep making that noise?" I ask.

"He's got breathing issues. Because his nose is so smushed," Mimi says.

"Aw. Poor Wart." I hold my arms open.

The dog jumps up excitedly and scrambles back onto the bed, walking all over my lap and almost falling over, he's so happy.

"I need to take him out," Mimi says, unzipping her sleeping bag and crawling out. She's wearing a big blue T-shirt with the word "SPAM" on it in yellow letters, and striped pajama pants and fuzzy pink socks. For the first time I notice that she's kind of small for a grownup. She's not that much taller than me, and she looks younger with her hair down. It's not quite shoulder length, and the ends curl in toward her face.

"Come on, Wart," she says, stretching her arms so that her elbows make little popping sounds. "You want to go potty?"

Wart jumps off the bed, lands heavily on the ground, and trots to the door.

"Be right back," Mimi says.

While she's taking the dog out, I get out of bed and look around the room a little more. I wrap my arms around myself to keep warm. The books piled against the walls are mostly library books, I guess the ones she was supposed to throw away. There are a bunch of copies of the Chronicles of Narnia and books by Madeleine L'Engle and Max Lucado and somebody named George MacDonald. There are some books for grownups too, like *Peace Like a River* and *The Power and the Glory* and *The Hiding Place*. I wonder if Mimi has read them all.

There's a big cardboard box in one corner of the room. When I peek inside it, I see a bunch of clothes. I guess she doesn't have a dresser.

I wander out of the bedroom and into a half living room, half kitchen as Mimi and Wart come back in. Wart bounds over to me to say hi like he hasn't seen me in a long time.

"Hey, Wart!" I say to him, scratching his back as he turns in circles, trying to lick my hand. "Uh, Mimi, where's the bathroom?"

"Around the corner and to the left," Mimi says.

When I get back, Mimi's standing in the kitchen half of the room, looking into her cupboard. I notice for the first time there isn't any refrigerator.

"Your toilet won't flush, and the sink isn't working," I tell Mimi. "I just used the hand sanitizer to wash my hands."

"Oh, sorry, I forgot to tell you the water isn't turned on," Mimi says. "There's actually a hole I dug outside that I use."

I stare at her. "You don't have water?"

"I have drinking water," Mimi says. She opens the cupboard under the sink and shows me rows and rows of old milk jugs.

"How do you take baths?" I ask.

"There's a barrel outside that fills up whenever it rains," she says. "I use it to fill up the bath tub."

"But it's cold!" I say.

"Yeah," Mimi says, making a face. "I take quick baths."

"Couldn't you heat the water up on the stove?"

"There isn't any electricity either."

"Why not?"

"Nobody was living here," Mimi says. "If somebody turned on the water and electricity, the government would notice. And besides, I can't use a credit card anymore. They'd be able to see the transaction."

I stand there for a minute, my eyes wide, not saying anything. I didn't think of any of that. I had kind of assumed that water and electricity just came automatically with the house. We really are completely disconnected? We have to poop outside?

Mimi leans against the counter. "Are you regretting coming here?"

I compare the cold little house with Mimi and the books and Wart to Grandma and Grandpa's, where it's warm and the toilets work, but Grandpa hit me and I have to go to school and see Dr. Snead and sleep in a room by myself. "No."

"Okay," says Mimi. She wraps her arms around herself and looks kind of like I do when I'm overwhelmed and worried. It's not very comforting to see grownups looking like that. "What do you want for breakfast?" Mimi asks.

I come to stand next to her and see what's in the cupboard. It's all stuff that doesn't need to be refrigerated— bagels and bread, apples, crackers, peanut butter, honey, cans of vegetables, chili, tuna, cookies, granola bars, raisins, trail mix, soup, prunes, bananas, and turkey jerky. I really want something warm and delicious for breakfast, but I don't want to make her feel bad by saying so.

"Can I make a peanut butter and banana sandwich?" I ask.

"Sure," Mimi says. "There's silverware in that drawer next to the sink and plates in the cupboard on your right."

We make ourselves some sandwiches and then go sit down on the living room carpet, since there isn't any table. Mimi brings two blankets in from the bedroom for us to wrap around ourselves for warmth, and the dog snuggles up next to me and snores.

We're both kind of quiet. Last night felt dangerous and exciting, running away. Now that I've escaped, I'm not sure what to do next.

"Do you think we can get my icon?" I ask through a mouthful of peanut butter.

"Your icon?" Mimi says.

"The one that did a miracle," I say. "I asked Father Innocent if he'd help me get it."

"We can probably do that," Mimi says. "Speaking of Father Innocent, where did I put my phone? I texted him last night that I was going to get you."

She gets up and starts looking through her purse on the counter. When she finds the phone, she pauses for a minute, reading something, and then comes and sits back down slowly. Her eyebrows are furrowed.

"What's the matter?" I ask. "Did he answer?"

"Yeah," Mimi says. "He's coming here. We need to get dressed and stuff as soon as we're done eating."

"He's coming here?" That seems like a good thing. So why does she look worried? "He isn't . . . he isn't going to make me go back, is he?"

"I don't know," Mimi says. "I might have done something really stupid." She stares at the last few bites of her sandwich on her plate.

I don't understand what she's talking about, but now I'm worried too. I try to finish my breakfast, and I have a hard time getting the sticky peanut butter down. When I'm done, Mimi takes my plate and her own and puts them on the kitchen counter.

We get dressed and cleaned up and put Wart away in his crate so he won't jump all over Father Innocent when he comes. Mimi brushes her teeth outside and spits in the overgrown bushes by the house, and I squirt some toothpaste on my finger and try my best to rub my teeth clean. I forgot my toothbrush at Grandma and Grandpa's house. At least my breath won't smell bad.

After that we sit on the porch and stare at the woods and the long gravel driveway, waiting for Father Innocent to come. It looks like the wood near the church trailer, and also the wood where I hid the St. Nicholas icon, but then again, all woods kind of look the same to me. We could be next to the school playground, for all I know. That makes me wonder about Alex Wesson and what he'll think if I'm not in school on Monday.

Finally a gold car comes into view at the end of the driveway and rattles towards us. Mimi stands up, so I stand up too, and we watch as the car pulls up alongside Mimi's beat-up white one. Father Innocent gets out, and then to my surprise, Daniel Liakos gets out of the passenger side. Mimi walks forward to Father, bowing to touch her right hand to the earth and then holding her palms out for a blessing. Father lays his hand over hers and blesses her. I stand awkwardly on the porch, not knowing whether to copy her or not.

"Let's go inside and talk," Father Innocent says. I can't tell what he's thinking. His beard hides his mouth, and his dark eyes are serious.

"I'm sorry there isn't anywhere to sit," Mimi says as we walk in. "Father, there's a bed in the other room, if you'd rather go in there."

"That's fine," the priest says. The grownups go into the bedroom, and I follow. Father Innocent sits on the bed—I really wish I'd made it before he got here—and Mimi and Daniel and I sit on the floor. I pull Mimi's sleeping bag towards me and stick my feet inside to warm them.

"So," Father Innocent says. "By now they'll have called the police. DRT will have been notified. Everyone Euphrosyne has talked about or been seen with in the past few months will be questioned. I've already warned the Wessons."

Mimi looks like she feels terrible. "Her grandfather was abusing her," she says. "I'm sorry, I just had to get her out of there."

Father Innocent turns to me. "He hurt you? Are you all right?"

"I'm okay," I say in a small voice. It was just a slap. I shouldn't have told anyone, just been tougher. Then Alex and his family wouldn't be in danger.

"You're sure?" he asks. "We need to take you to a doctor

if you're injured."

"It wasn't a big deal. I shouldn't have even said anything," I say, pulling the sleeping bag closer for security.

"It is a very big deal," Father Innocent says, and even though he isn't talking very loud, his voice is kind of scary because it's so serious. "It is a very, very big deal when someone hurts a child. Especially a child they should be protecting and caring for."

He pauses, staring into my eyes, and I'm not sure whether I'm supposed to say something or whether he's just done talking. I nod my head.

"But while I'm glad you're safe from your grandfather, Mimi taking you away has put you in maybe an even more dangerous position. I had hoped you could stay there safely until you were older, under the radar but still practicing Orthodoxy and maybe even recovering your icon. Now you've disappeared, and the fact that they haven't found you already will tell them that an adult is helping you. If we try to send you back to your grandparents' house now, they won't just watch you. They'll take you away and try to find out about us."

I glance at Mimi. She's staring at the wall and trying not to cry.

"So can I stay with Mimi, then?" I ask.

"This house is only temporarily safe," Father Innocent says. "Even Mary knows that. It's a matter of time until someone searches these woods or identifies a license plate or recognizes someone going out to get food."

I pull on my fingers and look from Mimi to Daniel, who so far hasn't said anything. "But then what can we do? Can we go to another country?"

"We don't have passports," Mimi says, still staring at the wall. "And they're watching the borders."

"Why do they hate us?" I burst out. "Who even are they? Why are they doing this? Why can't people leave us alone?"

"They call themselves the Neo-Emersonians," Daniel speaks up. "They've been gaining popularity for the past few years, speaking for pro-choice and same-sex marriage groups, criticizing the 'rigid intolerance' of Christians. They say the only sin is judging other people. Of course, they're judging and persecuting Christians—but then Christianity has always been targeted because it doesn't bend for society. And Orthodoxy is the very worst."

I remember Dr. Snead talking to me about my God being cruel and a God of hell, and him believing that the real God was the love and acceptance inside us. "How can they think they're doing the right thing by hurting us?" I ask. I think of the men shooting Mr. Liakos on the road.

"A wise man once said, 'I don't believe in God, and I hate him,'" says Father Innocent. "Some of them may be so deluded that they think they're doing what's right. I suspect most of them have latched onto Neo-Emersonianism because it justifies the hatred for God they already had. They're trying to destroy the religion that goes against their desire to do whatever they want."

I lean against Mimi. This is all a lot to process.

Mimi squeezes my knee through the sleeping bag. "What should we do with Euphrosyne, Father?" she asks.

Father Innocent breathes out a slow sigh. "I really don't know yet," he says. "Daniel has some contacts with people in Austria and has offered to try to reach out to them. If we could get the two of you out of the country, you would be safe."

"The two of us?" Mimi asks.

"The two of you," Father Innocent says. "You made a rather dramatic exit from the library. I don't think the Department of Religious Tolerance will let that slide."

Mimi looks embarrassed. "Oh. Right."

"And besides, Euphrosyne will need someone to watch out for her." Father Innocent gets up from the bed. "Daniel, you said you could get in touch with them this afternoon?"

"Yes," says Daniel. "Even if they'll help, though, how are we getting passports?"

"We'll cross that bridge when we come to it," Father says.

Which is what people say when they don't know what to do and thinking about it makes them even more worried.

"I'll see you two at liturgy tomorrow," Father Innocent says to Mimi and me.

Mimi stands up to get a blessing, and this time I bow and kiss Father's hand too, even though I'm nervous. His fingers are cool and clean and smell like hand soap.

Once Father and Daniel drive off, Mimi lets Wart out of his crate, and we stand on the porch for a few minutes and watch him sniff around in the yard.

"Always ask for a blessing before you do something big like kidnapping a twelve-year-old," Mimi says, staring into the woods.

January 14, 0001 ET

The next morning, Mimi takes a bath and then refills the tub for me to take one. When I put my hand in the water, it's freezing. There's no way I can get in that, even for just a few minutes. I stand looking stupidly at the tub, then decide that I can at least wash my hair. I dunk my head to get it wet, then rub Mimi's shampoo into it. It smells fruity. I rinse off and then wash my armpits with a soapy hand towel so I won't stink. Then I let the water drain out. I'm shivering really badly from my wet hair.

When I come out of the bathroom, I find Mimi burrowed under all the blankets and quilts on the bed.

"What are you doing?" I ask, my teeth chattering.

"So cold!" her muffled voice comes from under the covers.

"Me too!" I say. I get under the covers with her. She's wearing a long church skirt and a jacket, but her hands are still icy. We hug each other for warmth, which would normally be weird for me because I don't like touching people, except that I'm so cold I don't care, and Mimi's better than most grownups anyway.

"We need to go to church," Mimi groans after about ten

minutes, when it's finally starting to get warm under the covers.

"But it's *cold*," I remind her.

"We still need to go to church."

"But we could freeze to death."

"This is Alabama."

"It could happen."

"The church has a heater and a working toilet and sometimes hot coffee," Mimi says.

"Let's go."

It turns out the church is walking distance from Mimi's house. We trudge down the gravel driveway and then turn right on a footpath that cuts through the woods. After a few minutes of walking, my body starts to warm up, but my face is still cold, and my ears ache from the chill. I wish I had a headscarf like Mimi.

The path winds through the trees and between hills. In parts it's overgrown and we have to push branches out of the way. Leaves crunch under our feet. It takes about twenty minutes before we come out into the clearing with the trailer. A few cars are huddled together for warmth outside. Mimi and I climb the steps up to the door and walk in.

Warmth from the candles and heating units hit me. I breathe in the smell of incense and feel a shiver run up my spine. There aren't many people here this week. I don't see the Wessons, and I feel a guilty pang when I think they're in danger because I ran away. There are a few families, a few grownups standing by themselves. Father Innocent is in the altar, behind the panel of icons. Mimi and I venerate the center icon of Christ being baptized and then the front icons of Christ and the Theotokos. As I kiss the Theotokos's face and the face of Baby Jesus, the bells start to ring. The service is starting.

"Do you want to stand with me and sing in the choir?" Mimi whispers.

I shake my head. I can sing pretty well, but I get nervous doing it in front of people. And it's been a long time since I sang these songs. I don't remember all the words.

We back up quickly as Father comes out with the censer so we won't get in his way. "Are you sure?" Mimi asks. "Do you want me to stand with you, then?"

I shake my head again.

Mimi looks a little worried. "Okay," she whispers, poking my arm. "I'm right over here if you need me." She ducks her head and crosses herself as she walks in front of the center icon, then she takes her place next to Daniel and the other singers.

I back up to stand next to one of the families with little kids and wrap my arms around myself.

"In peace let us pray to the Lord," Father sings.

"Lord have mercy," sings the choir.

"For the peace from above and for the salvation of our souls let us pray to the Lord."

"Lord have mercy."

"For the peace of the whole world, for the good estate of the holy churches of God, and for the union of all men, let us pray to the Lord."

"Lord have mercy."

"For this holy House, and for those who with faith, reverence, and fear of God enter therein, let us pray to the Lord."

"Lord have mercy."

So many "Lord have mercy"s. For sailors. For travelers. For soldiers. For the sick. Even for the president. My mind starts to wander. The choir is small, but the voices blend together so well that it sounds like a bigger group singing. It's too big, too complicated a sound for just a few people. I peek to see if everyone around me is singing. Some of them are. Some are just standing silently, absorbing everything. I realize that my lips are moving and I've been singing along quietly without realizing it.

There's a little boy a few feet away from me, sitting on the toes of his daddy's shiny leather shoes. He's got blond hair and dark brown eyes, and he's playing with the buckles on his sandals. He catches me watching him and turns to hide in the folds of his dad's pant leg. I hug myself tighter and focus on the service again. I remember Dad picking me up and holding me sometimes in church when I got tired, before Kat came along. When I was the baby.

The choir sounds really beautiful. More beautiful than I've ever noticed, even back at St. John's, where there were a lot of people and all the Liakoses singing. When we sing "Holy God," I can almost pick out a harmony in the background that I never heard before. I glance over at Mimi, but she and the others are watching Daniel's hands as he directs, and they don't seem to be doing anything different.

When I notice the other priest in the altar, I can't remember whether he's been there all along and I just wasn't paying attention. He's helping Father Innocent like a deacon or one of the altar boys, but he's about a foot taller than Father Innocent and he seems . . . different. Brighter, or more colorful or something. I wish I could get a glimpse of his face. He's robed in red, not gold like the others, and he has a white stole with blue crosses draped around his neck and over one shoulder.

I look around to see if anybody else is surprised to see him.

The little boy with blond hair is staring at him wide-eyed. So is the baby that the woman next to me is holding. The two little girls in the back are pointing and whispering. None of the grownups seem to notice anything.

Now that I look around, though, there are strange people in the congregation too. More people than were here when liturgy started. It's weird—I don't notice them until I look away, and then I look back quickly and they're gone, but I remember seeing a flash of color or a face. Two of them, girls about my age, stand still enough for me to take in. One girl, maybe thirteen years old, has the longest hair I've ever seen, so long that it covers her shoulders and back and lies in dark curls on the floor. And beside her an older girl with her head covered holds a leafy cross in her hand.

Am I going crazy? Does nobody else see this?

No, the little blond-haired boy reaches out cautiously and

touches the dark curls with the tip of his finger.

The long-haired girl looks down and smiles at him. His parents don't notice anything. When the girl looks back up, her eyes meet mine, and her smile gets even bigger. She gives me a small wave.

I wave back shyly. She's different in the same way as the priest helping Father Innocent. When you look at her, it's like everything else seems pale and grey. Except the girl with the leafy cross beside her. They are both the most colorful things in the room, even though their dresses are brown and plain.

The baby in the arms of the lady next to me gurgles and reaches out his arms toward the long-haired girl and her friend. His mother bounces him gently and pats him on the back.

The priests and the altar boys come out for the reading of the Gospel, and I find myself standing behind the priest that I don't know. He smells like incense and something else—pine needles? I stare at the back of his red robes. The more I see him, the more I feel like I know him.

Father Innocent reads the Gospel.

"Glory to Thee, O Lord! Glory to Thee!" everyone sings.

Everything around me is getting greyer and greyer. Everything except the icons and the strangers. I can see them better now. They seem to fill every corner of the room. They're all different ages, some young, some old, their faces shining. Some wear crowns, many hold crosses in their hands. Some are dressed in rags, but they're so beautiful that the rags seem beautiful too. Can they see me? I look at my hands, and they are pale and grey compared to the strangers.

From far away I hear Father Innocent's voice as he begins the homily. Someone's hand is on my shoulder. I turn and see one of the bright people—a tall man with a shy face and messy brown hair and beard. He doesn't say anything, but smiles and pokes my nose with a callused finger, just the way my dad used to. He reaches into the pocket of his clean, white apron and pulls out something small and round that he presses into my hand. I uncurl my fingers and look at it. An

apple. Red and yellow, and as colorful as the bright people. I want to bite into it right then and there, but when I lift it to my mouth, the man shakes his head and points to the altar.

Father Innocent is talking to everyone, but his voice sounds like a muffled echo. Beside him stands the other priest, tall and shining. I suddenly remember my dream of the giant in the tree, the dream that made me find Father Innocent and start coming here. The tall priest turns to me, and I can see his face clearly for the first time.

It's him. There's no blood on his chest now, but I know it's him.

The girl with the long hair and the girl with the leafy cross take my hands. The man who gave me the apple kisses the top of my head, and then we leave the church.

It's like a dream. But it's too real. The January air is cold on my cheeks, and I can hear the crackle of dry leaves under our feet and smell the incense of the trees around us. The wind ruffles the long hair of the girl on my right and makes the leaves on the other girl's cross flutter against her hand. They know where we're going. They aren't afraid. When we step out of the trees and cross the dull blue pavement of a road, they don't even look for cars, just walk onward, their sandaled feet almost silent. When we reach the center line, they pause for a moment and look down at the pavement. I look too.

There's a dark stain. I don't know if it's really still here, or if I can see it because the bright girls are holding my hands, but I see it, and I look around me, and I know where we are. Because this is the place where Mr. Liakos died.

For the first time I lead them. We cross the road and re-enter the trees. Everything is leafless and colorless now, but I remember the green of leaves and the yellow Pascha sun as I ran barefoot, clutching the icon of St. Nicholas. Up a hill. Down a hill. To the place where the man shot at me, and farther on, to the creek where I spent those terrible few days that I try so hard not to remember, and finally to the leaning oak tree with the hollow trunk.

The two bright girls let go of my hands, and I walk forward. I reach my hand inside the hole, and my fingers touch smooth wood. I draw the icon out slowly. The tree has kept it safe from the rain—the dried trickle of blood is still there. I turn it and see my mom's handwriting on the back. It's the one thing I have of hers.

"Thank you," I say, turning around toward the bright girls.

But I'm alone in the woods.

"Hello?" I call out. "Hello?"

There's nobody there. Not even any sounds, except for a crow cawing somewhere in the distance. The colors of the trees and sky seem normal again. My hands holding the icon don't look grey anymore. The crusted blood is still on the icon. Other than that, everything seems normal. St. Nicholas's painted eyes stare at me without blinking.

Where am I? The road is behind me, I know that, but have no idea how to get back to the church. Was there a path to follow, or were we just walking through the woods? I can't remember. And it's cold. I wish again that I had Mimi's headscarf.

I hold the icon against my chest carefully so that I won't touch the blood, and then I start climbing the hill again to get back to the road. This place looks so different from the last time I was here.

When I get to the top of the hill, it's only a little way back through the trees. I have my head down as I'm trudging along, and the noise from the leaves under my feet is so loud that I don't hear the car until it pulls up in front of me. I jump back, scared.

It's a black sedan with a row of lights on the top and no markings. The passenger door opens, and Dr. Snead steps out.

"Hello, Hillary," he says. "I thought I might find you here."

SIX

January 14, 0001 ET — 12:33 pm

The back of the car smells like old sweat and smoke. I sit on the torn black leather and pull my fingers and stare at the denim pattern of my jeans. Dr. Snead and the driver are in the front, separated from me by a wall of glass. He took the icon, and now he's looking at it closely.

I thought they were going to ask me a bunch of questions, but so far Dr. Snead just said hi to me like I was in his office for an appointment. And then made me get in the car. I could have run. I probably should have run. But if they had searched the forest, would they have found the trailer? Or the house Mimi was hiding in?

I wonder what Mimi will think when she realizes I'm gone. I imagine her asking people if they've seen me, calling for me around the church, having to walk back to the house alone, not knowing what happened. Tears well up in my eyes, and I pull at my fingers so hard that it hurts.

Father Innocent said they'd ask me where I'd been and who'd helped me. *I'll never tell anyone*, I think to myself. *Never.*

Would Father and Mimi and Daniel believe that? Would they have to move the church or go into hiding?

The back of the car is so ugly and smelly, and I feel so

alone, that it's hard to remember how colorful and real the two bright girls looked, or St. Nicholas, or the man who gave me the apple.

The apple. I put a hand to my jacket pocket and feel something round and solid inside. Dr. Snead and the driver aren't paying any attention to me. I pull it out, and the flecks of red and yellow on its skin are just as rich as I remembered. I take a little bite. It's the best apple I've ever tasted, sweet and tart at the same time, so good that it tingles on my tongue. I chew and swallow it slowly and feel a little braver. I put the rest back in my pocket for later.

It's a long drive. We head back toward the city, driving past the McDonald's where Mr. Liakos ate his last breakfast, past neighborhoods and shopping centers, past the turn to get to Grandma and Grandpa's house, past the library and the school and through downtown, past Father Innocent's bookstore and the street that Dr. Snead's own office is on, all the way to a curved building with reflective glass sides and a duck pond in front. There's a huge metal sign facing the road that says "Department of Religious Tolerance."

The driver pulls around to the back of the building, and Dr. Snead makes me get out in front of a small brown door. I stand with my knees shaking as he punches in a code on the keypad next to the door to unlock it. I could run.

He leads me inside. The halls are bare, with white tiles and white walls and fluorescent lights. It smells like a doctor's office, which right away makes me even more scared. All the doors in the hall are windowless and closed. They have numbers, but no signs saying what's inside.

We take an elevator to the third floor and walk down a hallway that's exactly the same as the other one. Dr. Snead is still holding the icon under one arm, and I want to tell him to be careful with it, but I'm afraid if I say anything he'll start asking me questions. So I just follow him down the hall and around the corner to door 338. He holds it open for me and nods for me to go inside.

Whoa.

The walls are light pink, light blue, and light green, with murals of children and rainbows and school buses. The kids are the worst kind of cartoony—the terrifying kind with swollen fingers and huge heads and no noses. They're all dressed differently, some wearing hippie clothes with peace signs, some with bright red *A*s on their shirts, a couple with five-pointed star necklaces on. There's a big sign that says "Children's Department" in bubbly orange letters, and under-neath it is a sliding window and receptionist's desk like in a dentist's office. It's too warm, and it smells like rubbing alcohol.

Dr. Snead puts a hand on my back and steers me toward the receptionist. There are a couple of other people waiting in chairs, mostly nervous-looking grownups, and I can feel them watching us.

"This is Hillary Matthews," Dr. Snead tells the reception-ist. "We need to see Dr. Wilcott as soon as you can squeeze us in."

"Alrighty," the receptionist says cheerfully. She looks a little older than Mimi and has a boy cut and purple bangs. She's got one of those star necklaces on like the kids in the murals. She types something into her computer and then smiles. "He should be with you in a few minutes."

Dr. Snead steers me again to a chair and sits down next to me. Nobody's offered me anything to drink or a chance to go to the bathroom. I'm scared to ask.

The lady in the chair next to me is pregnant. She's got one hand over her stomach protectively, and she keeps looking at me in a scared way. I wonder if she's waiting for her kid.

It's not very long before the door to the back opens and a man in a suit comes out. "Hillary?" he calls.

It's the man from the library. Pink skin, white hair, fancy suit. The one I saw taking Boston out of school.

"Come on," says Dr. Snead, getting up.

The man from the library leads us to a room with a table and three chairs. There's nothing else except a huge mirror set into one wall. There are no cheerful colors or murals in here, just white walls and white tiles on the floor. Dr. Snead and Dr. Wilcott sit in two chairs on one side of the table, and I have to sit facing them. Dr. Snead lays down the icon in the middle of the table so that St. Nicholas is staring up at the sickly white lights.

No one says anything. They just watch me and wait. It's terrifying having two grown-up men stare at you silently for so long.

"Have you told my grandparents?" I ask finally.

"They'll be notified," Dr. Snead says.

More silence. I know they want me to get nervous and start saying stuff. But this is like the staring match I had with Dr. Snead. And I won that. I can sit here as long as they can and not say anything. Just watch me. I kind of have to go to the bathroom, so I'll probably pee in my chair eventually, but I'm not saying anything.

Dr. Wilcott breaks the silence. "Is there blood on that thing?" he says suddenly, frowning at the icon.

"It was that way when we found it," says Dr. Snead.

Dr. Wilcott pulls it towards him and turns it over. "Her mom's?"

"I assume so. Hillary went to a lot of effort to get it back."

Dr. Wilcott nods. "Tell me, Hillary," he says. "Who is this a picture of?"

I hesitate, but I don't see how this could give anything away. "St. Nicholas," I say finally.

"Like Santa Claus?" Dr. Wilcott asks.

"Yeah," I say.

"This doesn't look much like Santa Claus," he says with a smile. "He certainly doesn't look very jolly."

He turns the icon towards me, and I see St. Nicholas's stern eyes and set mouth.

I don't say anything, just shrug. If Santa isn't fat and dumb-looking, I don't see that as a bad thing.

"I thought Christians weren't supposed to worship things like this," Dr. Wilcott says. "Graven images. Isn't that kind of like idolatry?"

It's like a picture of a friend, I think. *Not an idol*. But if I get drawn in, I might say too much, so I just say, "I don't know."

Dr. Snead chuckles. "Same old Hillary, shutting herself off."

He leans forward and lays his hands on the table. I make myself look back up. I can see all the little dots on the skin on his nose, and every strand of slicked-back hair. "We're not in my office anymore," he says quietly. "The rules have changed somewhat.

"I was hoping you'd understand, Hillary," he goes on. "I thought you were starting to realize that the lies and legalism of Christianity just lead to violence. But it looks like you've made your choice. So I have to ask—who helped you get your icon back?"

"Nobody," I say.

"You walked all the way from your grandparents' house to the woods?" Dr. Wilcott says skeptically. "That's about an hour-long drive."

"Was it the Wessons? Carter and his family?" Dr. Snead asks.

"No," I say.

We sit in silence for a few minutes. Dr. Snead is watching me like he's trying to decide what to do.

"Remember the rules have changed, Hillary," he says. "This isn't school, this isn't a game. There are consequences for telling lies."

"I want to go home," I say shakily.

Dr. Snead ignores me. He stands up and puts the icon back under his arm.

"That's mine," I say.

Dr. Wilcott stands up too. He adjusts his expensive suit and checks his watch. "Your recommendation?" he asks Dr. Snead.

"Whatever you think is best," Dr. Snead says. He glances at me. "I'd take a direct approach. She's stubborn."

"The classroom is full," says Dr. Wilcott. "It'll be thinned out tomorrow, though. I'm going to put her in Cell 14 for tonight."

Dr. Snead nods. "See you tomorrow, Hillary," he says. And then he leaves, and it's just me and Dr. Wilcott.

That's it? No more questions?

"Come on," Dr. Wilcott says to me, checking his watch again.

I could fight, but he's a lot bigger than me. So I stand up and follow him out the door. He leads me down a few more hallways that all look the same and finally to a metal door with an electronic keypad. He types in the code, and we go through.

It's completely black inside.

"Always forget, every time," Dr. Wilcott mutters to himself. He reaches back through the door and flips a switch. Light floods the huge room, and I hear people cry out.

The room is as big as a warehouse and divided up into small glass cells, each about as big as an office cubicle. Most have kids in them, kids around my age, who huddle on the floor, covering their eyes with their hands. I wonder how long it's been since the lights were turned on.

Dr. Wilcott takes me by the arm and pulls me forward, past the first row of cells and to an empty one labeled "14." I hesitate when he opens the door for me, and he pushes me inside impatiently.

"Wait!" I say. "I need to go to the bathroom."

He shuts the glass door and says something that I can't hear, pointing to the corner of the cell. There's a small hole cut out of the floor. But no toilet paper. When I turn back to him, he's already walking away towards the exit.

"Hey!" I yell, pounding the glass with the side of my fist. "Hey, come back!"

He either can't hear me or ignores me. I see the metal door slam behind him, and then the lights go out.

January 15, 0001 ET

Have mercy on me, O God, according to Thy great mercy, and according to the multitude of Thy compassions, blot out my transgressions. Wash me thoroughly from my iniquity and cleanse me from my sin, for I know my iniquity and my sin is ever before me. Against Thee only have I sinned and done this evil before Thee, that Thou might . . . and prevail when Thou art judged. For behold, I was born in iniquity, and in sins did my mother bear me, for behold Thou hast loved truth, the hidden and secret things of Thy wisdom hast Thou made manifest unto me. Cleanse me . . . sprinkle me with hyssop and I shall be made clean, wash me and I shall be whiter than snow, make me to hear joy and gladness, the bones that be humbled they shall rejoice . . .

My brain is stumbling over the psalm when I wake up on the cold tile. Some of it I can't remember at all, and some of it I'm probably getting wrong. I can hear Dad's voice reading it during evening prayers, but that was so long ago. I used to know it all by heart.

Something is hurting my side. I roll over and feel around blindly in the dark. My fingers find something hard and round. The apple.

I haven't had anything to eat or drink since the bagel and peanut butter I ate at Mimi's house before church. I don't know if that was today or yesterday, but my stomach hurts and my mouth is dry. I eat the apple as slowly as I can. I even eat the bitter part in the middle. Everything besides the seeds and the stem. My hands are sticky with apple juice, so I lick them clean. The sound of my chewing is the only thing that breaks the silence. Which is kind of creepy, since I know there are other kids in cells all around me.

I crawl over to one of the glass walls and tap on it with my fingernail. I wait for a few minutes and then tap louder. Nothing. It's like I'm completely alone in the dark.

There's nothing to see, nothing to hear, nothing to do. I use the hole in the corner of the cell awkwardly and then curl up in a ball by the door and think of black planets and colorless towns—places where you have to fit in, to stop believing, or bad things happen to you. Did Mimi somehow know I would end up here? Is that why she gave me all those books to read?

I think of her and the pig dog Wart sitting alone together in the cold house. I hope they're okay. I hope I'll be okay.

January 16, 0001 ET

When the lights come on, I shriek and hide my face in my arms.

It's worse than when your grandma switches on your light on a winter morning to get you out of bed, worse than when your little sister shines a flashlight right in your eyes to be funny, even worse than when you get your eyes checked and then have to go into a sunny Alabama parking lot. I literally can't raise my eyelids. They refuse to move. Even the red glare coming through my skin is painful. I sit paralyzed until the door of my cell opens and hits me in the back of the head.

"Ow!" I cry, curling up into a tighter ball.

Strong hands grab me under the arms and lift me to my feet. I almost fall over again, I'm so dizzy from thirst and from not being able to see.

The pair of hands jerks me back upright and spins me to face the door. "Come on," says the woman's voice. She doesn't sound very nice. "Come on, walk. I'm not carrying you."

I stumble towards her blindly, and she sighs. She puts one hand on my shoulder and grabs my hair with another, twisting her fingers so that it hurts. I can hear other kids being pulled out of their cells. Somewhere a little girl is crying. The woman pushes me forward and uses my hair to steer me to the exit. I still can't open my eyes. I try, but my eyelids just flutter.

It's loud and chaotic in the hallway. Sounds of crying, complaining, and begging bounce around and confuse me. The woman holding my hair isn't careful about steering me, and a few times I bump into people or trip over their feet. They take us around a number of corners, and with the noise and not being able to see, I'm too distracted to pay attention to direction.

The walk is long enough and the light in the hallway is dim enough that, by the time we stop, I can crack open my right eye for a few seconds at a time. The other kids around me are dirty and thin. Two or three of them are crying and need tissues bad.

We've stopped in front of a door. It opens, and I squint at Dr. Wilcott. A girl next to me, about Kat's age, whimpers.

"Welcome to the classroom," Dr. Wilcott says to us. "Come, take your seats, and we'll start learning."

Inside, the classroom is a lot like Miss Linda's room. There's a dry-erase board, posters on the wall, and rows of desks. The only thing different is that the desks look funny and there's a water fountain by the dry-erase board. I swallow dryly. I'm so thirsty. The woman holding me by the hair pushes one hand between my shoulder blades and pulls my head back with the other so that I have to walk to desk number fourteen with my back arched. I clench my teeth to keep from crying like the little girl.

The desks have flat tops with weird metal things on each side, shaped almost like cuffs. The woman shoves my arms into them and then flips the top pieces of metal closed so I'm trapped. My hands can move, but my forearms are locked to the desk. Right away a strand of hair starts to tickle my cheek, and I can't do anything about it.

"Thank you, ladies," Dr. Wilcott says when all the kids are locked to their desks. The women who dragged us in there walk out, and we're left alone, blinking at the doctor as our eyes adjust.

Dr. Wilcott takes a tissue from his desk and wipes the runny nose of the girl in desk number four. "What's your name?" he asks her gently.

She looks terrified. "G-g-grace," she stutters.

Dr. Wilcott raises his eyebrows in concern. "Are you sure?" he says. "I thought your name was Miley. That's what your papers say."

Grace or Miley opens her mouth, but no sound comes out.

"Are you thirsty, Miley?" the doctor asks.

She nods shakily.

"Say 'yes sir.'"

"Y-y-yes sir."

"I'll tell you what, Miley," says Dr. Wilcott. "If you can

come write your name, your *real* name, on the board, I'll let you have a drink of water. Does that sound good? You can use whatever color marker you want."

The girl nods.

Dr. Wilcott pulls a small black remote from his breast pocket. He points it at the girl like she's a TV set, and her cuffs fall open with a *clunk*.

She stumbles to the front. She's so skinny that her arms look weird as she reaches for the red marker. Like her skin doesn't fit her anymore.

She lifts the marker and hesitates. The water fountain is right beside her, shining and silver. It hums cheerfully.

M

I

She stops, biting her lip.

Dr. Wilcott watches her silently.

Her hand moves to the eraser, hovers for a second, then goes back to the board.

L

E

Y

"Very good, Miley," Dr. Wilcott says. "You may have five seconds at the water fountain. One. Two. Three. Four. Five."

Miley gulps as much water as she can. She runs back to her seat. Some of the kids look at her jealously. Others look disgusted.

Dr. Wilcott clicks the remote again, and her cuffs close. "There are two rules in my classroom," he says to us. He uncaps a green marker and writes squeakily on the top of the board. "Rule number one: Learning is rewarded. Rule number two: Always raise your hand."

He chuckles and erases rule number two. "Sorry, bit of light humor there." He clears his throat and rewrites: "Rule number two: Lies can hurt."

"Any questions?" he asks us.

Nobody says anything. Miley needs another tissue.

"Excellent," says Dr. Wilcott. "Then let's begin with introducing ourselves. Number One, will you start? Just your name and age."

Number One is a boy about my age. "Connor," he says. "I'm eleven."

"Very good, Connor. You may have five seconds at the water fountain."

Connor gets to go up and drink water.

"I'm Graylin," says Number Two. "I'm nine."

Graylin also gets water.

Number Three has a stubborn look on his face. "I'm John," he says. "Fourteen."

"Are you sure, John?" Dr. Wilcott says.

"Yes," says John.

"All right then. Miley, we already know your name. How old are you?" he says, turning away. John doesn't get any water.

I want water so bad. The kids who get it come back looking relieved, brushing drops from their lips and sighing. Numbers Five and Six get water. Numbers Seven and Eight don't.

And that's when John starts to yell.

"Ow! Ow, stop! Make it stop! Please!"

"What's the matter, John?" Dr. Wilcott asks calmly.

Seven and Eight look warily at John as he pulls frantically at his cuffs. "It's hot! Please, stop! Stop it!" he yells. He squeezes his eyes and his fists shut, sobbing. Then he stops, breathing hard. He stares at his desk.

What on earth just happened? I didn't see anything change. Seven and Eight look scared. Dr. Wilcott goes on to Nine, Ten, and Eleven. They all get water. When he asks Number Twelve her name, she has to repeat herself twice because Seven starts screaming and then Eight is yelling too. They twist and jerk in their desks.

Twelve and Thirteen both get water.

"Number Fourteen?" Dr. Wilcott asks, looking at me expectantly.

I hesitate.

"Number Fourteen, what's your name?"

"Euphrosyne," I say finally. "Age twelve."

"Well, that's a strange name," is all Dr. Wilcott says. "Number Fifteen, name and age?"

Number Fifteen is a ten-year-old boy named Mitchell. He gets to drink water, but he looks sad.

Dr. Wilcott goes and sits behind his desk, turning on his computer. I know it's coming. Maybe he's waiting for it, because I see him glance at me. I clench my fists and take deep breaths.

My metal cuffs get warmer and warmer. So hot that I

open my mouth to scream like Number Seven, but then close it again and lay my head down on my desk, squeezing my eyes shut and tensing all my muscles as my arms burn. It lasts for about five seconds, the same amount of time I could have been drinking water. Then the cuffs cool again. I keep my head down.

When I finally sit back up, everyone's eyes are on me.

"Are you all right, Euphrosyne?" Dr. Wilcott asks.

I nod, unable to speak.

"You're sure your name is Euphrosyne?"

I close my eyes and nod again.

The pain returns.

"Euphrosyne used to be what was called an 'Orthodox' Christian," Dr. Wilcott says. I can barely hear him over the ringing in my ears. "Have any of you heard of them? No? They thought some Christians were better than others. They painted pictures of them, worshipped them. They thought the Orthodox were better than everybody else and that God loved them more.

"Do you think you're better than everybody else?" Dr. Wilcott asks me. "Are you better than Miley and Mitchell?"

I bite my tongue until I taste metal, and finally the cuffs cool again. "No," I whisper.

"Do you think you're special, Euphrosyne?"

I struggle to breathe evenly. And I remember the icon stopping the bullet, and me seeing St. Nicholas and the long-haired girl and the girl with the cross. And getting the apple from the man with the messy hair and beard. "Yes," I say.

Dr. Wilcott shakes his head. "Why would you think that?"

"Maybe I'm supposed to do something."

"You're twelve years old," says Dr. Wilcott. "Do you think you're going to save the world?" He smiles at me like grownups do when kids say something cute, and then he goes back to his desk.

"Let's talk about Jesus," he says. "Jesus was a real man, a historical figure. But was he the son of God? Number One—Connor—what do you think?"

Connor turns to look at me and then looks back down at his desk. He doesn't say anything.

"Connor?" Dr. Wilcott prods.

Connor's lips are trembling. I can't see his eyes because his dirty blond bangs are so long and ragged, but I'm pretty sure he's about to start crying.

Dr. Wilcott bends over to peer through Connor's bangs. "If Jesus was God, why did he die? Why couldn't he save himself?"

Connor mumbles something.

"Ah. Connor says that 'he died to save us,'" Dr. Wilcott tells us. He straightens back up and paces between the desks. "But who did he save us from?"

Connor looks confused. So do a lot of people.

"He died to keep God from sending people to hell, didn't he?" asks Dr. Wilcott. "Does that sound like a loving God? A God that would kill his own son?"

Everybody's quiet. I know there's something wrong with what he's saying, but I can't think straight because my arms hurt so bad. I give my head a little shake.

Dr. Wilcott sees.

"You disagree, Number Fourteen?" he asks quickly.

Please don't. Please, I don't want it to hurt again. "God . . . didn't kill Jesus," I say heavily. "People did."

"Isn't that the same thing, though?" Dr. Wilcott asks. "God is all-powerful, right? Everything goes according to his plan? So if Jesus died, isn't it God's fault?"

I can feel the cuffs start to warm a little. I can't think. I can't think and I can't remember, and everyone's looking at me, but if I can't be brave, then no one else will, and maybe that's why I'm here. "We . . . can make . . . choices," I say. "To do bad things . . . or good things. God lets us . . . do that."

"Ah, you believe in free will," says Dr. Wilcott, nodding.

I don't know what that means. The cuffs are still only warm, but the heat on my burned arms hurts worse than anything I've ever felt.

"Tell me, though, Euphrosyne," says Dr. Wilcott. "What about all those places in the Bible where it talks about pre-destination? And the elect?"

He's using big words, and my brain won't focus. I don't remember. I can't think. "Jesus . . . loves . . . me," I say through gritted teeth. It's not an answer. It's the only thing my brain can come up with.

"If he loves you," Dr. Wilcott says softly, bending down like he did in front of Connor. "If he's powerful and he loves you, why are you here?"

I can't talk because the cuffs are hot now and I'm opening my mouth and screaming silently.

"Who helped you run away, Euphrosyne?" he asks. "Where are they?"

Mimi. I picture her shelving books at the library, pulling up in the car to take me away from Grandpa, sleeping on the floor while I slept in her bed. I put my forehead on my desk.

"Where are they, Euphrosyne?" Dr. Wilcott asks. "Why didn't they take care of you? Why doesn't God take care of you?"

"He does," I say, my voice cracking.

Dr. Wilcott laughs. I can't see him with my head down, but I hear the rustle of his suit as he stands up straight and starts to pace. "Is anyone taking care of Euphrosyne?" he asks the other kids.

The cuffs start to cool. The pain stays.

"Believing that there's some God who's going to take care of you is like believing in Santa Claus," he says scornfully. "This is the real world, children."

Somewhere in his talking I lose track of what's happening, and everything goes fuzzy and dark.

January 17, 0001 ET

I throw up in my cell. I manage to get to the hole in the corner in time. Not a lot comes out anyway, just a little bit of liquid. I gag a couple more times, but there's nothing left in my stomach. I'm shaking and covered in sweat. It's so hot. And my arms are on fire. I want to scream, they hurt so bad. I can't see them in the dark, and I'm afraid to touch them. I lie on my back on the floor and try to hold them off the ground so that nothing rubs against the burns.

Lord Jesus Christ, have mercy on me.

Lord Jesus Christ, have mercy on me.

Lord Jesus Christ have mercy on me Lord Jesus Christ have mercy on me Lord Jesus Christ have mercy on me Lord Jesus Christ have mercy on me LordJesusChristhavemercyonme LordJesusChristhavemercy-onmeLordJesusChristhavemercyonmeLordJesusChristhavemercyonme . . .

Holding my arms up hurts. Letting them rest on the floor hurts.

Nobody can hear me in here. I cry for a while and feel bad for crying, because I'm so thirsty I hate using water for tears.

When the lights come on, I can't get up, even when the woman kicks me with her boot. I just lie on the floor with my eyes closed and say the Jesus Prayer. Finally she goes away.

Things get swimmy and dark again, which is good, because my arms don't hurt as much when it's like that. I hear voices and feel people touching me and lifting me, but I try to stay under the surface.

I don't know how much time has gone by when I can't keep away any longer and I have to open my eyes. I'm lying in a bed. And there's a tube stuck in my arm. Two people are talking.

"He says he's here for a Hillary Matthews? Says he's her father."

"Alex Matthews died last April."

I know that second voice—Dr. Snead.

"So I should tell him to leave, Doctor?"

"No, no. Absolutely not. Send him up." A pause. "He's alone, you say? Make sure you check his bag and pockets before letting him through."

"Yes, sir."

Footsteps walking away.

Suddenly Dr. Snead's face is right above me. I jerk backwards and yelp.

"Sorry to scare you," says Dr. Snead apologetically. "I just wanted to check on you. How are you doing?"

My arms are on fire. Maybe the rest of me too. I close my eyes and try to go back to being unconscious.

"I don't think you really need this anymore," Dr. Snead says, and I feel him pull the tube out of my arm. It would normally have hurt, but I barely notice it. "My, you're running quite a fever," he says, laying his thick hand on my forehead.

I want to tell him to stop touching me. To leave me alone. Why am I here, anyway, instead of in the classroom? It's almost exactly like his old office. Nice furniture, framed quotes on the walls, a fake potted plant. And the St. Nicholas icon lying on his desk. My eyes stop on it.

"Yes, I've been having a good look at that," Dr. Snead says, following my gaze. "A very nice reprint of the original. I had the blood tested too—it was a different type from yours.

Whose blood is that, Hillary? Your mother's? Or someone who was helping you?"

"My name is Euphrosyne," I say. My lip is so dry that it splits a little when I open my mouth.

Dr. Snead shakes his head. "I thought you'd have gone with Hillary after yesterday," he says. "According to Dr. Wilcott, you weren't very helpful."

When I don't answer, he goes on. "*I don't know*," he says in a fake-high voice. "It doesn't matter," he says in his normal voice. "Your father will tell us more than you could have anyway."

My dad?

There's a knock on the office door. The receptionist lady with the boy-cut hair and the five-pointed star necklace comes in. Behind her is an older man with a beard and a black cassock. It's Father Innocent. The receptionist shoots him a scared look and ducks out of the room as quickly as she can. Then she scurries back in.

"Here's what was in his briefcase," she says, dropping a Ziplock bag on the desk and then making her escape.

Father Innocent and Dr. Snead just stand there watching each other. It seems wrong for them to be in the same building, maybe even the same world. They're like characters from two different books showing up side by side. I saw Hershey almost get in a fight with another dog once, and it looked like this. They both just stood there glaring at each other with the hair on their backs sticking straight up.

"Are you all right, Euphrosyne?" Father Innocent finally

asks in a low voice.

Dr. Snead smirks like he won something and saunters around his desk to sit in his swivel chair with hands folded.

"Yeah," I say, which is a lie. A pretty obvious one, since I'm lying here on a gurney with my arms all burnt.

Dr. Snead picks up the Ziplock bag and dumps the stuff out onto his desk. "*The Power and the Glory?*" he asks Father Innocent, picking up a worn paperback and turning it over. "Ironic. At least you're not a drunk though, as far as I can see."

"Neither am I Catholic," says Father Innocent, keeping his eyes on me. "I didn't know you read Christian literature."

Dr. Snead gives a short, dry laugh. "There you are," he says. "Always ready to judge others."

"It is a fault of mine," says Father Innocent, bowing his head. "But it is mine, and not Orthodoxy's."

"I'm sure," says Dr. Snead. "So. I assume you're here for one of these?" he waves his hand from me to the icon. "Or both?"

"Both," says Father Innocent.

"How about we make a deal?" says Dr. Snead. "I'll give you one. You choose."

"Then I must take Euphrosyne."

"The sick orphan instead of a holy icon? Look at her. She won't make it out to your car."

"There are two holy icons here," says Father.

Dr. Snead blinks in confusion.

"And I believe St. Nicholas can take care of himself," Father

Innocent says. "I'm a bit tempted to follow his example."

"What do you mean?" Dr. Snead asks.

"I would like to punch you in the face," Father Innocent says very seriously.

Dr. Snead pales. Father Innocent is a big man. "You're in a government building," he says. "With security. You wouldn't dare. I don't even know how you expect to get out of here."

I'm starting to feel sick to my stomach again. How *does* he plan to get out of here? Doesn't he know we're both trapped now?

"I expect you to let us walk out of here," says Father Innocent.

Dr. Snead laughs. "And why would I do that? We have you now. A priest. What's left of Orthodoxy here revolves around you and counts on you. With you gone, they'll fall apart. And you can give us all their names, all their secrets. It was incredibly stupid of you to come here."

"I expect you to let us walk out, James, because I know you," Father says.

For a minute I forget the burning in my arms and look from Father Innocent to Dr. Snead in shock. They know each other?

"You may not think I remember a young altar boy whose elderly parents were very hard on him. The altar boy who became a teenager and quit coming to church, who got involved with drugs and other young men, who joined the radical secularists and rose in their ranks. But I remember James."

Dr. Snead is even paler now. Maybe it's because he's so angry.

My mind is reeling. Dr. Snead was Orthodox? But that explains all the things he knew, about fasting and Pascha and what my parents believed.

"Nearly everyone has religious roots," Dr. Snead says. "No one will care if you tell them."

"That's not why you'll let us go."

"No? Then why would I?"

"Because I think you remember too, James," says Father Innocent. "You've been in the altar and tasted the Host. You hate everything about that world, but you remember, and you know. You know what that icon on your desk is, however much you try to deny it, and you know what the child is. And you know what I am. And what fate you will meet if you go against us now."

Dr. Snead stands very still with the muscles in his jaw clenching and unclenching. His eyes shift to the icon of St. Nicholas, and I know he's thinking about the blood that doesn't match mine, and the bullet hole that didn't go all the way through the thin wood.

Father Innocent doesn't wait for him to decide. He walks heavily to the bed on wheels where I'm lying and scoops me up in his arms. I'm tall for my age. I can feel his arms shaking. He kicks open the door of Dr. Snead's office and walks out, through the blank hallway, through the waiting room with the creepy murals, and into the main hall.

"That won't work for very long," he says to me, breathing heavily and breaking into a lumbering run toward the elevator. "We need to get out before he changes his mind. Is anything hurt besides your arms?"

"No," I whimper. "But there are other kids—they're going to hurt them—"

"We'll figure something out," he pants. "First we need to make it out of here alive. Tap that button for me, please."

I kick the elevator button with my foot and it glows orange. All the movement is making me dizzy, and my arm that's touching Father Innocent's cassock hurts so bad that I start to cry, leaving dark, wet splotches on his chest.

The elevator door opens, and Father carries me in just as a door down the hall opens and Dr. Snead comes running out. "Stop!" he yells, starting toward us.

The elevator door shuts in his face, and we drop downward.

We wait while we sink lower and lower, and I can hear Father Innocent saying the Jesus Prayer to himself.

"We didn't get the icon," I say through my tears.

"I couldn't carry both of you, and your arms are hurt," says the priest.

I cry harder at the thought of leaving St. Nicholas there with Dr. Snead and Dr. Wilcott.

When the elevator opens, Father Innocent steps out and starts to run towards a blue sign that says *Lobby*. I hear footsteps and shouting behind us, but I can't see past Father's shoulder. There's a loud *crack* that leaves my ears ringing, and another three gunshots as we turn a corner into a fancy lobby with tiled floors and ugly paintings.

"Wait! Wait, sir!" cries the receptionist, standing up behind her desk. "You can't—"

Father Innocent turns and rams through the swinging glass doors with his back, then through a second set of doors, and we're outside, running toward a white car with a familiar face behind the wheel. Mimi. She looks terrified, but I see her mouth my name.

Father Innocent opens the back passenger door as four security guards burst out of the building. He turns around to angle me inside, and for half a second I see the guard point his gun at us. I have a strange moment of déjà vu. Then another gunshot splits the air.

SEVEN

Blessed art Thou, O Lord, teach me Thy statutes.

The choir of Saints has found the source of life and the door of Paradise; may I too find the way through repentance; I am the lost sheep, call me back, O Savior, and save me.

Blessed art Thou, O Lord, teach me Thy statutes.

You Holy Martyrs, who proclaimed the Lamb of God, and like lambs were slain, and have been taken over to the unending life which knows no aging, plead with Him to grant us abolition of our debts.

Blessed art Thou, O Lord, teach me Thy statutes.

All you who trod in life the hard and narrow way; all you who took the Cross as a yoke, and followed Me in faith, come, enjoy the heavenly rewards and crowns which I have prepared for you.

Blessed art Thou, O Lord, teach me Thy statutes.

I am an image of Thine ineffable glory, though I bear the marks of offenses; take pity on Thy creature, Master, and with compassion cleanse me; and give me the longed-for fatherland, making me once again a citizen of Paradise.

Blessed art Thou, O Lord, teach me Thy statutes.

Of old Thou formed me from nothing and honored me with Thy divine image, but because I transgressed Thy commandment, Thou returned me to the earth from which I was taken; bring me back to Thy likeness, my ancient beauty.

Blessed art Thou, O Lord, teach me Thy statutes.

—EVLOGITARIA FOR THE DEAD

The First Day

It only hurts for a second, and then I'm gone. I rush through buildings and trees and fields and more trees, and through a boarded-up door that I almost recognize and into a dark house. And there I stop.

It's quiet. Nothing moves.

"Hello?" I call, frightened. But no sound comes out of my mouth. "Father Innocent?" I try to say. "Mimi?" I can only hear the words in my head. What's happening? Where am I? Why can't I talk?

I am too overwhelmed by everything that's happened. I can't do this. I lean back against the wall and sink to the floor. When I draw my legs up against my chest, I can't see my knees at all. I can sense them, but it's like I'm invisible. I start to cry again for what feels like the millionth time.

It takes me a while to see the teenage boy. He starts as a faint glow and gets bigger and brighter until I stop crying and stare at the person sitting next to me. I'm so surprised that I can't even say anything.

The teenager smiles at me. He's a lot taller than I am, even sitting down, and he has curly chestnut hair pulled back into a ponytail. If I weren't so upset, I'd probably be jealous of his hair. It's prettier than any girl's hair I've ever seen. In fact, *he's* better-looking than any girl I've ever seen. I can't help staring. He's got on jeans and a red jacket, and something belted around his waist that's poking me.

"It's a sword," he says.

"What?" I say, and even though my voice doesn't make any sound, he still hears me.

"It's a sword," he says again. He unbends his legs and twists to pull the sword out of its leather case-thingy. Even though the light in the room is dim, the blade glows with a pearly light.

"The case is called a scabbard," he says, like he can tell what I'm thinking.

"Can I hold it?" I ask.

"You can try," says the teenager. "I don't think you'll be able to now, though." He holds the blade lightly in his hands so that I can take it by the handle.

I reach one of my invisible hands to grasp it. For a second I feel the cold metal against my skin, but then my hand slips through it like I'm a ghost.

"Better than most souls," the teenager grins. "Must be

because of the apple. And anyway, you're special."

"Why can't I touch things?" I ask shakily. "Why can't I see my hands?"

The teenager's face gets serious. "Don't be scared, okay?"

That's never a good sign. "What's wrong with me?" I whisper.

The boy pats me on the shoulder. Even though I can't touch things, he can still touch me. Weird. "You're—well—you died. Only your body, though," he adds quickly. "When that security guard shot you."

"I'm *dead?*" I ask squeakily. I'm in danger of crying for the million-and-first time.

"Only your body," says the boy. Like that makes it okay or something.

"Am I a ghost?" I ask.

"No," the boy says, laughing like I said something funny. "You're a soul."

"Then—am I going to heaven?" I'm afraid to ask about the other possibility.

"That's not up to me," says the boy. "But you lived well. I'd be hopeful if I were you. The Lord sees the heart and all that is in it. And you are His child."

"If I'm just a soul, why do I have an invisible body, then? And who—who are you?"

The boy puts his sword back in its case and bends his legs again so he can rest his elbows on his knees. "You spent twelve years living in a body," he says. "Your soul is still kind of body-shaped."

That makes sense in a weird way. "But who are you?"

"I'm Shamar," he says. "I'm your guardian angel."

Right away I remember the icon that used to hang between my bed and Kat's, of the curly-haired angel in blue robes and a red cloak, the one carrying a sword.

"So you've been here all along?" I ask.

Shamar nods. "Ever since you were baptized."

"You were old enough to be a guardian angel then?" He can't be more than seventeen or eighteen years old.

"I'm a lot older than I look," he says with a smile.

"Oh." It's weird to think he's been watching me my whole life. I think of all the stupid things I've done, all the times I was mean to Kat or whined to Mom and Dad. It's kind of embarrassing.

We sit quietly for a minute and listen to cicadas outside the house. The windows are boarded up, and I can only see the room dimly in the light coming through the cracks in the wood.

"Where are we?" I ask finally.

"Don't you recognize it?" asks Shamar. "It's your old house."

Even though I don't have a real body, I still feel a shiver run down my spine. He's telling the truth—now I recognize the shape of the living room. This is where Dad and Hershey died. Are they still here?

Shamar gives my arm a squeeze like he knows what I'm thinking. "Everything was cleaned up, and the house was closed months ago," he says quietly. "There's some furniture and stuff left, but nothing that will hurt you to see. Want me to make it light in here?"

I nod silently and take his hand with my invisible one. I expect him to start glowing brighter or something. Instead he flips the light switch on and helps me up.

The living room is almost empty. Our old couch is still sitting sadly against the back wall, and there's some broken glass left on the floor. That's it. The icons are gone from the walls, and the icon table in the corner and the hanging oil lamp have disappeared. Shamar and I walk to the place where I remember Dad and Hershey lying, and I look down at the floor. All the blood is cleaned up.

"Is Dad—did he go to heaven?" I ask.

"Yes," says Shamar firmly.

I feel some warmth inside me. "What about Mom and Kat?" I ask.

"Yes, they've been praying for you," he answers.

"I want to go there," I say softly. "Can we go now?"

"Not yet," he says. "You have three days left here, and then you begin your journey. But I'll be with you the whole time."

I squeeze his hand for comfort.

We walk through the hallway and stop at the door to the room that Kat and I shared. The walls are still pink. The curtains are gone, and the sheets and covers have disappeared from the beds. And all our toys. There's nothing under my bed. Under Kat's I find a folded piece of paper that someone overlooked. I try to pick it up, and my fingers go through it.

"Can you help me?" I ask Shamar.

"You know you can't take it with you," he warns.

"I just want to look at it."

Shamar bends down and gets the paper. He unfolds it for me to see. It's a Valentine's Day card with pink and purple hearts that I drew for Kat three years ago. I didn't know she'd kept it all this time. Shamar folds it gently and puts it back under the bed.

"You know, she spent her three days with you," he says to me.

"She did?" I ask. "When I was in the woods?"

He nods. "Your mom and dad did too. They love you very much."

We go into Mom and Dad's room. The curtains and sheets are gone in here too. I don't want to look under the bed because I don't like to remember hiding down there. Someone has spray-painted weird stuff on the walls, and there are a couple of crushed beer cans in the corner. I remember all the Saturday mornings when Kat and I would sneak in here and pull Dad out of bed to make pancakes. He would cling to the headboard as Kat and I pulled on his feet, and Mom would burrow under the blankets and tell us all to go away, and that having kids was the biggest mistake she ever made. But she'd always give me a big hug when I'd tell her I'd brought her coffee.

Is it going to be the same in heaven? It can't possibly be the same, not after everything that's happened. Besides, they've been together almost a year now without me. Do they still think about me?

"They pray for you every day," says Shamar. It's creepy how he seems to know what I'm thinking.

I lie down on Mom and Dad's bed and hug my arms around my invisible self. The mattress doesn't bend at all underneath me.

Shamar takes the sword and its case off his belt and lies down beside me. I cuddle up against him and think that this is what it must be like to have a brother, if your brother is thousands of years old and an angel and wiser than you could ever imagine.

"Do you want to go anywhere else today?" Shamar asks.

I want to know what happened to Mimi and Father Innocent and the Wessons. But right now I want to stay here. So I shake my head.

"Okay," Shamar whispers.

After a minute I ask, "Do souls sleep?"

"You don't need to," he says. "You can if you want to, though. I'll keep you safe."

I close my eyes and let myself drift.

The Second Day

When I wake up, the sun is streaming through the curtainless windows. It should be cold inside, but I feel warm. Whether that's because of Shamar's arm around me or because I don't technically have a body, I don't know.

His eyes are already open. Or maybe he's been awake the whole time. When he feels me move, he gives me a little squeeze. "Are you rested now?" he asks.

"Yeah, I think so." I look around the room at the graffiti on the walls and the bare windows. This doesn't seem like Mom and Dad's room anymore. I'm ready to go.

Shamar sits up. "Where would you like to go today?" he asks.

"I want to see Mimi and Father Innocent," I say. I try to sit up too and then realize something's different. I don't feel heavy any more. It's like I'm in water. I'm not even sure that I'm touching the bed, because I can't sense my legs. I remember where they should be, but there's nothing there.

"I feel weird," I say to Shamar. "I feel more like a ghost."

Even though I'm not solid anymore, Shamar still manages to hug me. "You are not a ghost," he reminds me. "You're a soul. I know this is scary, but it's not permanent."

"Have you ever died?" I ask him.

"No," he says, smiling. "But my Master has. Every pain you have felt, He has already known. And He's made a home for you."

I picture a little house with Mom and Dad and Kat waiting for me. I don't know if that's what it will be like, but it makes me feel better.

"We should get going," Shamar says. "You don't want to waste your time here."

"How long will it take us to get there?" I ask.

"Almost no time at all," he says. "You ready?"

"Yes."

The room seems to spin for a second and then dissolves around us. We're in the woods, standing next to the clearing where the church trailer rests. Well, Shamar is standing. I'm sort of floating.

There are two cars that I recognize parked by the trailer. One gold, one white. The white one has a window missing and some little round holes in the back door. The license plate is gone.

"Is Mimi in the church?" I ask Shamar.

"Yes," he says. "And Father Innocent."

"Does that mean—am I in there too?"

"Your body is inside," Shamar says. "*You* are here, with me."

I float a little closer to him. "Will I have to see me if we go in?" I ask. My voice is high-pitched like it always is when I'm scared. I try to pull on my fingers, but I don't have any.

"No. They've put you in a coffin," Shamar says. "Tomorrow is your panikhida. You'll be buried with honor."

"Okay," I say. I'm still scared, but I want to see Mimi. I want to make sure she's all right.

We cross the yard and climb the stairs to the porch. I wonder if they'll be able to see Shamar. I can hear him and see him as if he were a normal human. What would they think about a teenager with a sword coming in?

Shamar goes straight through the door without opening it, just like I do. It's almost as if the door moves aside for him. And then we're in the church.

The only light is a few candles. Someone's put them in

the sand trays in front of the icons of Christ, the Theotokos, and St. Nicholas. There's a wooden box in the middle of the room, and I can see someone sitting in front of it with her head shrouded and her knees drawn up to her chest.

"Mimi?" I say.

"She won't be able to hear you," Shamar says. "She may sense you, though, if you get close enough."

I float towards her. Shamar stays behind, watching silently.

She's the first human that I've seen since I died. When I get close, I realize I can see more than just the stuff on the outside. I can see her soul too. And it makes me sad. Its silver glow has dark scars across it. There's a jagged rip over her heart and another on her right hand, the hand she's holding over her face as she cries. The one across her heart looks old, but the one on her hand is fresh. I hover beside her, trying to touch her.

"Lord have mercy, Lord have mercy, Lord have mercy," she whispers over and over again. She makes the sign of the cross, and her fingers leave a trail of light that lingers for a moment before disappearing. On the ground next to her is a wrinkled piece of paper. It's the picture I drew for her for Christmas, with her standing next to all the book characters.

"Lord have mercy, Lord have mercy," she whispers.

I want so much to hug her and tell her that I'm okay. I drift forward so that I'm where she is, hovering in the same space she occupies. Her crying slows a little. She keeps praying, and I can feel her breathing grow steady. We sit there for a while.

Father Innocent comes in. I don't notice him until he's right next to us, getting down on the floor beside Mimi with some difficulty. There are some scars on his soul too, mostly healed. Lines of light glow faintly from his forehead to his stomach and across his shoulders, like he has made the sign of the cross so many times that it's drawn there permanently.

Father picks up the piece of paper and smooths it in his hands. He smiles a little when he sees the picture, even though his eyes stay sad.

Mimi crosses herself again and grows quiet, staring at the coffin.

"She made this for you?" Father asks in a low voice.

"For Christmas," Mimi says. "She drew it. She was a good artist."

"She loved you," says Father Innocent.

"It would have been better if I'd left her alone," says Mimi. She wipes tears from her eyes. "If it hadn't been for me, she wouldn't have died."

No, I want to say. *It wasn't your fault!*

"If it hadn't been for you, she might have given up on her faith," Father Innocent says. "She died a martyr's death. And her body stopped that bullet from killing me."

Mimi shakes her head. "She was only twelve. She was too young to make that sacrifice."

"She was older and stronger in many ways than either of us," says Father Innocent. "Euphrosyne was special. Maybe because her family died, maybe because the saints helped her. They prepared her for what she had to do."

"What do you mean? That she was destined to die?" Mimi asks.

"We're all destined to die," Father says. "But Euphrosyne was sent to be a light. And she was strengthened for that purpose."

"You make it sound like she was Jesus," Mimi says.

"She wasn't our Lord and Savior, the Son of God," says Father Innocent. "But the saints are in Christ, and Christ is in us, and through the Holy Spirit, they help us."

"Do you think Euphrosyne was a saint?"

"It's not for me to say. God determines saints, not men. I do know that she was stronger than any twelve-year-old child ought to have been. You saw those burns on her arms. Not many adults can go through pain like that without breaking."

"And there was the icon," Mimi says.

"Yes. There was the icon."

"Why did St. Nicholas save her once, though, if she was only going to die later?" Mimi asks, shaking her head.

Father Innocent is silent for a few minutes. He stares at the wooden box, and his eyes look glassy.

"I don't understand it all," he says finally. "She saved my life, but I would rather have died than have a child take a bullet for me. I didn't want that trade. There's something deeper that happened, though, something that makes me think it was meant to be this way. That it was about Euphrosyne, not me."

"What?" Mimi asks.

"St. Nicholas."

"You mean the icon?"

"The *icons*."

Mimi looks confused. "There were two of them?"

"Two icons," Father Innocent says thoughtfully. "Two shooters, two bullets, two icons. We are all created in the *eikon* of God, the image of God. Did Euphrosyne ever tell you of the miracle that saved her when Reader Mark was killed? She held the icon in front of her chest . . ."

I'm trying to understand what he's saying when I hear Shamar call for me. I slip away from Mimi and back to where he's standing at the door.

"We need to go," he says. "Your grandmother needs you."

The church spins away and dissolves around us, just like my old house did. This time it takes longer for the world to settle back into place.

Shamar and I are in a familiar driveway, in front of a familiar house with perfectly pruned bushes and no trees. Grandpa's truck and Grandma's car are both in the driveway, and Uncle Robert's fancy blue sedan is parked on the street. I know the wind is blowing, because I see it shake the leaves of the boxwood and tug on Shamar's curls. But I can't feel it anymore.

"I don't want to go in," I whisper.

Shamar doesn't say anything.

I stare at the living room window. I can see the light of the television flickering inside. Do they know I died? They have to know by now.

I remember Grandma reading to me when I was sick and baking cookies with me. Shamar said she needed me.

"You'll go with me, right?" I say finally.

Shamar nods. "I'll be right beside you. And they can't see you."

"Okay."

We go slowly up to the front door. The Winter Holiday wreath is still up. I guess nobody remembered to take it down. The wood of the door seems to make way for us as we go through, just like it did going into the church.

Inside, everything is the same as I remember it. No one has taken the tree down. There's a football game on the television, and Grandpa, Uncle Robert, and Aunt Cindy are all sitting around watching it. Grandpa's eyes look glazed and unfocused. There's a pile of empty cans beside his armchair.

Shamar looks weird in here, all otherworldly and angelic in the dim yellow light. His sharp profile and the long fingers on the handle of his sword don't belong in the same room as Grandma and Grandpa's dingy curtains and the half-eaten box of pizza on the coffee table. I feel more like a ghost than ever with the two of us watching the others invisibly. Uncle Robert takes another slice of pizza and turns back to the game.

Where's Grandma? The light in the kitchen is off. I take a last look around at the living room and then float up the stairs. Shamar follows behind me.

It seems empty. I float into Grandma's room first, but it's empty except for the clothes on the floor (which is weird, because she's usually really clean) and the pile of battered romance novels on the dresser. Her bathroom is dark. The guest room is dark, too. The only room left for her to be in is mine.

Shamar is waiting for me. He somehow hugs me—I don't know how you can hug someone without a body—and we turn to my door.

Nothing has moved since I ran away. There's a pile of books and papers on the floor where I emptied out my backpack, and some of the drawers of the dresser hang halfway out from when I was grabbing clothes. My clock ticks calmly. Grandma lies on the unmade bed, curled up into a little ball. She looks smaller and older than I've ever seen her. She doesn't have any makeup on.

"Is she okay?" I ask Shamar.

"No," he says quietly. "She might be, though, in the end. I don't know how things will turn out."

Grandma's soul doesn't have as many scars as Mimi's had, but it seems dimmer. Like a candle in a jar that's stained with smoke. Maybe it's because she's older, maybe not. I float forward to hover in the same space she lies in, just like I did with Mimi. As soon as I do she starts to cry. She shakes silently and covers her mouth to keep everybody downstairs from hearing her.

"You're sure I can't talk to her?" I ask Shamar. It hurts so bad to see her like this. She wasn't my parents, but she was nice to me. She was special to me.

"You can pray for her," Shamar says.

So I say the Jesus Prayer over and over again. Shamar comes next to us and lays a hand on her shoulder. If she can feel it, she doesn't show anything. A sob escapes her mouth, and she reaches to grab my pillow and press it against her face. Something's underneath it.

Grandma lifts her head as her hand brushes the book. She wipes her eyes and pulls it towards her. *A Wrinkle in Time.* The last book I read. She opens it and runs a finger across the inside front cover where I wrote my name. Not Hillary. Euphrosyne. I must not have been thinking.

Another tear runs down Grandma's cheek. "Euphrosyne," she whispers.

I pause in the middle of the Jesus Prayer. Is she talking to me or just reading out loud?

"I'm so sorry, honey," she murmurs, hugging the book against her. "I'm so, so sorry." Grandma lays her head back down on the bed and shuts her eyes.

I forgive you, I think to her.

Grandma gives a long sigh and then her breathing steadies. I go back to saying the Jesus Prayer. After a while I hear her snoring softly.

"Do you want to go somewhere else?" Shamar says after a few minutes, when I stop praying.

"Not yet. I want to stay with her."

"All right."

So we stay for a long time, even after we hear Uncle Robert and Aunt Cindy's car pull out of the driveway and the sun goes down and the moon shines in through my window on the broken Nativity figures on the floor. The television stays on all night long, and I never hear Grandpa come upstairs.

In the morning Grandma stirs and looks around in confusion. When she remembers, pain runs across her face, and I think she's about to cry again. She sits up and rubs her forehead.

Lord Jesus Christ, have mercy on Grandma, I think.

Grandma slowly gets up from the bed and looks at the clock. She limps towards the door, then stops as something catches her eye. Sunlight glitters on the pieces of Baby Jesus and the Theotokos. She reaches down and picks a piece up.

It's the face, neck, and shoulders of Baby Jesus. He smiles up at Grandma.

She stares at the piece in her hand for a long time. I can't tell if she's happy or sad or angry. Her hand closes into a fist over the porcelain and she glances toward the door. There's no sound from downstairs but the television.

Very slowly she brings her hand up to her forehead and then down to her stomach, then across her shoulders. She has a shocked look on her face, like she can't believe what she just did. She can't see the glowing lines of the cross that she's drawn. But she stands a little straighter.

The Third Day

There's one last thing that I have to do before I go.

I can feel myself changing. I feel older. Not like a little kid. Maybe dying does that to you, or maybe once your soul is just a soul and not part of a body, age doesn't matter so much anymore. I'm not a different person. I'm still Euphrosyne. But it's like all the selfish and insecure feelings that come along with being a twelve-year-old are fading away. Shamar doesn't look as old, even though he was around thousands of years before I was made. I wonder if Mom and Dad feel younger in heaven. And what Kat looks like.

Shamar leads me through the sterile hallways and the lobby with the hideous paintings of noseless children. We pass security guards, businessmen, and nurses. None of them see us. Some of their souls are barely more than shadows. They all seem more worried and stressed than I've ever seen grownups. Did I just not notice before?

I stop for a minute in front of the door that leads to the dark room with the cells. "Can we help them?" I ask Shamar.

"That's not the task we've been given," he says.

That sounds cold. "But we can't just leave them here."

"There is a plan," Shamar says more gently. "There is hope for them. As you have been taken care of, so shall they be taken care of."

"You mean they all *die?*" I ask.

"Almost all humans die," Shamar says. "'Do not fear those who kill the body but cannot kill the soul.'"

He can't understand. He's never died before.

"I haven't died, but my Lord has," says Shamar.

I wish it wasn't so easy for him to guess what I'm thinking.

"There is hope for them," Shamar says. "You've already given them a light. They won't be abandoned here. There are others like me assigned to them."

It's hard to walk past that door. I believe him, though. And before we go on, he gives me a little smile and turns on the light switch. "Next time they'll be ready," he whispers.

Dr. Snead isn't in his office.

I don't know whether I'm disappointed or relieved. There's a good chance that I'll never have to see him again.

The icon of St. Nicholas is on his desk, lying between my file and a heap of legal papers. "Can you pick it up for me?" I ask Shamar.

"I think you'll be able to this time," he says.

"But I don't have a body. I can't feel anything anymore."

Shamar lifts the icon and holds it out towards me. "Take it," he says. "It saved your life."

I have no hands to take it with, no way to hold it. But when Shamar lets go, it somehow stays with me. Like it's connected to my soul.

"You can't bring it with you when we leave for good," Shamar says, just like he did when I wanted Kat's piece of paper. "What will we do with it?"

"Put it somewhere safe," I say. "Until someone else needs it."

"And where would that be?"

I think for a minute. "The library," I say. "Nonfiction. Once it gets lost in there, it's impossible to track down."

Dr. Snead's office crumbles away.

Leaving

I can hear Mimi's voice, and Daniel's and Father Innocent's. And lots of others. It's as though they're coming from far away.

Lord have mercy . . .

"It's time," says my guardian angel.

He's not wearing jeans and a jacket anymore, but blue robes and a red cloak. His sword is out, and he looks less human, more giant.

Lord have mercy . . .

"Stay close to me," says Shamar.

"I will," I say. I'm terrified and excited all at the same time.

For the ever-remembered handmaiden of God, Euphrosyne . . .

The world melts away.

Chapter One:

1. How is Euphrosyne's new room at her grandparents' different from her old room? Who do you think is responsible for the difference, Euphrosyne or her grandmother? How do the changes reflect Euphrosyne's new identity as Hillary?

2. What are some reasons that finding empty shoes on St. Nicholas Day might be particularly hard for Euphrosyne? Why is she mad at herself when she finds them empty? Have you ever gone through something like this, and if so, how did it affect you?

3. What are some details about Dr. Snead that suggest he's not just looking to help Euphrosyne cope with her grief? Are there certain things he says that you agree with, or would agree with in another context? Why?

Chapter Two:

1. Dr. Snead claims that the new government isn't really anti-Christian, just anti-prejudice, and that removing religion is just a prevention of violence triggered by Christian intolerance. What are some of the problems with his argument? Is he entirely wrong?

2. Why does Euphrosyne feel the need to rescue what she can of the Nativity set?

3. Is Mimi right to give Euphrosyne directions to the bookstore downtown? What would you have done in her place, and why?

Chapter Three:

1. After meeting Father Innocent, Euphrosyne struggles with anger and confusion over why God saved some people from death and not others. Her appointment with Dr. Snead leaves her feeling numb, but seeing the snow and stars that night seems to help her. Why do you think that is, and have you experienced anything similar?

2. How do some aspects of Orthodoxy show up on Winter Holiday? Do you think that some things can become Orthodox without their maker's intention or full understanding? If so, what are some examples?

3. Aside from missing her family, why doesn't Euphrosyne like the new Winter Holiday? How is Winter Holiday like Dr. Snead's version of God?

Chapter Four:

1. What are some signs that Euphrosyne's grandma really does care about her and want the best for her?

2. How is liturgy different for Euphrosyne after everything that has happened? Do you think the absence from church had any hidden benefits for her?

3. What are Grandpa's reasons for getting angry with Euphrosyne? How would he see his actions as justified, and do you think Grandma would agree?

Chapter Five:

1. How does Euphrosyne's attitude change after her grandpa hits her? Why does she cuss for the first time in Dr. Snead's office, and why does she regret it?

2. Was Mimi right to rescue Euphrosyne from her grandparents' house? Do you think she may have had any

other motivations (conscious or unconscious) for taking Euphrosyne? What do you think would have happened if she had left Euphrosyne there?
3. Who are the bright people Euphrosyne sees in the liturgy? Why do you think the man with messy hair gives her an apple?

Chapter Six:

1. Describe the inside of the Department of Religious Tolerance. How is it different from the church trailer? What makes it so frightening for Euphrosyne?
2. How are Dr. Wilcott's tactics for arguing against Christianity different from Dr. Snead's? Why do you think they take different approaches?
3. What is Euphrosyne's moment of *déja vu* at the end of the chapter?

Chapter Seven:

1. After Euphrosyne is shot, she finds herself back at her old home. Why do you think her soul returns there, even though her family is gone?
2. When she visits Mimi and Father Innocent, Euphrosyne sees scars and bright lines on their souls. What might these symbolize in real life? How do they relate back to the Evlogitaria for the Dead at the beginning of the chapter?
3. What does Father Innocent mean when he says that there were two icons? Why doesn't he think it was a coincidence that Euphrosyne died the way she did?
4. How will Euphrosyne's death change the world she left behind?

an article by Georgia Briggs

THERE ARE STORIES WE READ that leave lasting imprints on our brains. They stick with us all of our lives, stronger for some of us than our own memories. Not all words have this effect. I have probably forgotten ninety percent of what I've read in my short lifetime, but a few core books, a few fragments of story, have become so important to me that they now form a crucial part of who I am.

The fact that our brains latch on to stories isn't surprising. We are lingual beings, called into existence by the divine Logos and molded from dust into repositories of experience and memory. What fascinates me is the way some tales become universally absorbed, while others become intrinsic parts of only a few individuals.

Some books are beloved by everyone. C.S. Lewis believed that the reason for this was that the best art reflects Heaven. The stories resonate with us because something in us recognizes their truth and beauty. In his book *The Great Divorce,* a citizen of Heaven reasons with an artist who has gone astray, "When you painted on earth—at least in your earlier days—it was because you caught glimpses of Heaven in the earthly landscape.

The success of your painting was that it enabled others to see the glimpses too."

This is, of course, a Christian perspective, and some would argue bitterly against a universal truth or an immutable beauty. Many movies and books written nowadays glorify the idea that beauty is entirely in the eye of the beholder. Whatever the individual likes is beautiful, even if no one else in the world agrees with him. Every person is unique, and therefore there are as many types of beauty as there are people.

The problem with this is simply that the evidence points otherwise; there are some things that everyone just loves. We have bestsellers. We have famous works of art. We have thousands of people dressing up in cloaks and pointy hats waiting in line at Barnes and Noble for the newest Harry Potter release. Although we are unique, we are all human and created in the image, the ikon, of God. We share DNA whether we like it or not, and in smaller circles we share languages, cultures, and the earth on which we live. We may brag that no one is the same—and it's true that no one is exactly the same—but the fact remains that we are cut from the same cloth, and that shows up in our art and literature. We are drawn to similar things. We are drawn to truth and beauty.

This all makes sense from a Christian perspective.

It's natural that stories revealing truth speak to us as part of God's creation. What is more surprising is that within the vast body of work revealing truth, God goes even farther and uses specific pieces of art and literature to shape us as individuals and call us to Him. Maybe I focus on this aspect because I'm a Westerner and prone to consider the individual rather than the group, or maybe it's just part of my human limitation. I see the world through my own eyes and no one else's. The omnipotent and omnipresent God has the sole capability of seeing us simultaneously as individuals and as a group.

Anyway, it's amazing to me that God has used literature in my life specifically. Some books I read, like *The Chronicles of Narnia* and *Harry Potter*, I know to be universally beloved, and my affection for these works has provided me with a strange and precious connection with others. Other books I read were special to me, but not to everyone. Most people I met who read these stories enjoyed them, but the words didn't resonate as deeply with them as they did with me. A few books that come to mind are *Till We Have Faces* by C.S. Lewis, *Deerskin* and *The Hero and the Crown* by Robin McKinley, *Jane Eyre* by Charlotte Brontë, and *I Capture the Castle* by Dodie Smith. These particular stories rang true for me, partly because of my personality and partly because of the things I was going through at the time. I have met a few people who connect with them the same way I do, but not many.

Over the years I've realized that each one of these special books contained elements of God's calling for me. My church, my patron saint, my struggles with health, and even my marriage were foreshadowed in these books. Perhaps that's why they struck me so deeply when I first read them. God was planting a desire in my heart for the good things He had planned for me.

What books have been the most meaningful to you? Are they popular or obscure? How have they changed you or your life?

—from the author's blog post
https://georgiabriggsauthor.wordpress.com/
2016/12/19/books-that-stay-with-us/

GEORGIA BRIGGS lives in Birmingham, Alabama with her family and a pig-like Boston terrier. When she isn't writing or studying iconography, she enjoys baking cookies and singing along with recordings of Russian men's choirs. Georgia is a member of Saint Symeon Orthodox Church in Birmingham.

Ancient Faith Publishing hopes you have enjoyed and benefited from this book. The proceeds from the sales of our books only partially cover the costs of operating our nonprofit ministry—which includes both the work of **Ancient Faith Publishing** and the work of **Ancient Faith Radio.** Your financial support makes it possible to continue this ministry both in print and online. Donations are tax-deductible and can be made at **www.ancientfaith.com.**

To view our other publications,
please visit our website: **store.ancientfaith.com**

Bringing you Orthodox Christian music, readings,
prayers, teaching, and podcasts 24 hours a day since 2004 at
www.ancientfaith.com

www.ingramcontent.com/pod-product-compliance
Lightning Source LLC
Chambersburg PA
CBHW061438210726
48287CB00007B/2261